THE
PLAYBOY PRINCE
OF SCANDAL

THE
PLAYBOY PRINCE
OF SCANDAL

SUSAN STEPHENS

MILLS & BOON

First published in Great Britain 2021
by Mills & Boon, an imprint of HarperCollins*Publishers* Ltd,
1 London Bridge Street, London, SE1 9GF

www.harpercollins.co.uk

HarperCollins*Publishers*
1st Floor, Watermarque Building,
Ringsend Road, Dublin 4, Ireland

Large Print edition 2021

The Playboy Prince of Scandal © 2021 Susan Stephens

ISBN: 978-0-263-28861-2

05/21

MIX
Paper from
responsible sources
FSC™ C007454

This book is produced from independently certified
FSC™ paper to ensure responsible forest management.
For more information visit www.harpercollins.co.uk/green.

Printed and bound in Great Britain
by CPI Group (UK) Ltd, Croydon, CR0 4YY

For my readers.

There's nothing better than reading and music to lift the mood. I hope you enjoy reading this book even more than I enjoyed writing it, and that the happy-ever-after ending gives you the type of happy feeling that stays with you until you pick up your next romance.

With my love to you,

Susan xx

CHAPTER ONE

*The Winter Palace of Prince Cesar
Romano di Sestieri Ardente, Isla Ardente*

'SOFIA ACOSTA? Are you serious?' Cesar speared a look at his long-suffering equerry, Domenico de Sufriente. Dom had been reading out the proposed guest list for Prince Cesar's annual banquet celebrating the start of the polo season, to be held at Cesar's *palazzo* in Rome.

'Signorina Acosta should be invited with her brothers,' Dom pointed out, 'or you risk insulting the entire Acosta family.'

Cesar frowned. That would not do. He planned to play exhibition matches in aid of charity with the Acosta brothers' Team Lobos in various locations across the world. Working out a way to exclude his least favourite woman without offending her brothers was impossible. It couldn't be done.

Dom cleared his throat to attract Cesar's attention. 'You expressed a wish to field a mixed team for your next charity event. Having grown up in competition with her brothers, Sofia Acosta is—'

'Don't mention that woman to me!'

'One of the finest riders of her generation,' Dom ventured.

'But not a professional rider like her brothers,' Cesar pointed out.

'True, but there are few who can match her on the field of play.'

After the furore she had created, Sofia would pull in the crowds, Cesar silently conceded. The exhibition matches would benefit all his charities. 'Her skill on horseback is undeniable, but I'll never forgive her for what she did.' Using his hand like a blade showed his feelings on the matter.

'The article?' Dom proposed mildly.

'Of course the article.' What Sofia had written was the most florid pack of lies, and with her by-line brazenly plastered over the rubbish in a newspaper belonging to Cesar's old adversary Howard Blake. He'd been at odds with the man since their schooldays, when

Blake had stopped at nothing to get some innocent fellow student to take any blame directed at him—until he'd tried it on with Cesar. That hadn't gone too well for Blake, Cesar recalled.

What was the relationship between Blake and Sofia? Was she another innocent dupe, playing a role in some new tactic Howard had thought up to bring Cesar down to repay him for policing Blake during their years at school? Was it possible Sofia hadn't realised the harm the article could do to her family and to his? Why target him at all? They met in passing at polo matches, so why had she set out to destroy his reputation?

He only knew the woman through her brothers, though he'd registered Sofia's face and figure, as both were outstanding. Was she in cahoots with Blake? Without knowing the facts, he could rule nothing out. There was only one certainty, and that was that he refused to dignify her smut with a response.

'I will deal with Sofia Acosta in my own time.'

'Yes, sir.'

Dom bowed his head, but not before Cesar

had caught sight of the expression on his equerry's face. 'Why are you looking so smug, almost as if this pleases you? You're lucky that you still have a job—that anyone in the palace has a job. Sofia Acosta tried to bring us all down, so please don't suggest she has any finer qualities. She's a typical over-achiever, dipping her snout into multiple troughs because she can't bring herself to keep it out. I applaud dynamism, but not when the only possible motive is profit.'

'She rides like a demon,' Dom reminded him.

'Perhaps you would too, if you'd grown up in a horse-mad family.'

'I doubt it,' Dom murmured beneath his breath as he straightened his perfectly straight tie.

'Regrettably, she would be an asset to the team,' Cesar added, musing out loud. 'She'd draw the crowds based on her scandalous nib-dipping alone.'

Money-grabbing siren, he raged inwardly. Sofia Acosta might have the face of an angel, and a body made for sin, but it seemed to him that she'd stop at nothing, even bringing down a country, if it stood in the way of her lining her pockets.

A warm breeze chose that moment to steal in through an open window. It went some way to softening his tension, by reminding him of what lay outside the palace. However luxurious—and Palazzo Ardente was exquisite—a palace was just a set of rooms, static and unchanging, while the ocean and the beach were fresh and new every day.

'Just don't put that woman anywhere near me,' he instructed as he left his desk.

'The banquet will be held at your *palazzo* in Rome where there is a very long dining table...'

'Excellent. I will sit at the head, while Sofia will be at the far end with my mother and sister.' The hint of a smile tugged his hard mouth. 'I'd like to see Signorina Nib-Scribbler lecture them on the error of my ways.'

Sofia Acosta, outstanding polo player, amateur artist and sometime journalist, had famously written an article about European royalty, mostly featuring Cesar, though she had also taken a passing swipe at her brothers. The headline banner had screamed, 'Is

Royalty Necessary in Today's World?' The piece had caused a storm on social media. As an ex-Special Forces, polo-playing billionaire prince, Cesar had been put under the microscope—Sofia's fantasy microscope. His reported success with women, according to her, had made him sound more like a rampaging satyr than a dutiful prince.

She'd found numerous archive shots, showing him in every form of undress: playing polo bareback, barefoot, in banged-up jeans, topless, with a bandana tied around his head, making him look more like a kickboxer on vacation than a serious-minded working royal. There was even one of him naked beneath a waterfall, slicking back his hair as if he had nothing better to do than idle away his time in a tropical lagoon.

Granted, a few shots showed him in his official capacity, but always with an array of different women on his arm.

Had there really been so many?

The upshot of it was that a playboy billionaire, more intent on womanising and indulging in a hedonistic lifestyle than leading his country, was as far away from the man he was as it was possible to imagine. Duty came first. Now. Then. Always.

Not to say he had no appetite for pleasure, but that was then and this was now, and he always looked forward. Sofia Acosta had dredged up the past, embroidering the facts until they could only cast doubt in people's minds. What he found almost harder to believe was the way she'd dragged her brothers through the same mire. So much for family loyalty!

Why should he forgive Sofia Acosta for making him and his friends of many years the butt of her argument when she hadn't given him the courtesy of seeing her words before they had gone to print? The effect on his pride might have been fleeting, but the longer-lasting effect on his country, and on the trust of his people, was what he cared about. Had she thought of that before she had put pen to paper? He doubted Sofia Acosta had thought of anyone but herself.

And now he was expected to sit in the same room as this woman and make small talk with her?

'Sofia Acosta won't be the last unwanted

guest you are forced to welcome,' Dom pointed out, reading Cesar's mind with his customary ease. 'Think of this as a trial run for the many unpleasant duties you'll face in the years to come.' Dom turned the page in his notebook. 'You requested a meeting with Sofia's brothers and your sister Olivia after the formal dinner?'

'Correct.' Anything to avoid dancing with the twittering princesses his mother and sister had no doubt seen fit to invite.

'And Sofia Acosta will be included as well?' Dom pressed diffidently.

'She will have to be included,' he reluctantly agreed. He frowned. 'That's supposing we can drag Signorina Acosta away from her hippy commune.'

'The facility is more of a retreat,' Don ventured as he handed over a report, 'funded entirely by Signorina Acosta.'

'With money inherited from her parents?' Don confirmed this.

'So, the demon rider has some redeeming features,' he murmured as he scanned the report Dom had offered for him to read.

'This is my decision,' he stated. Unfolding

his athletic frame from the chair, he went to stand by the window. 'I will meet with the Acostas, including Sofia Acosta, and my sister Olivia, after the state dinner while the other guests are enjoying dancing to the orchestra.'

'A wise decision, sir.'

Dom had his head down, but why was he smiling? What was his equerry thinking? Recently, Cesar had begun to doubt Dom's advice, because something had changed in his manner. His equerry wasn't as open as he had used to be.

Before he could progress his thoughts, a pair of sparkling black eyes invaded his mind. They belonged to a voluptuous woman who could throw any man off his game. It was hard to avoid Sofia Acosta when they attended polo matches across the world, and when their paths crossed there was always fire between them.

There'd be no fire at his dinner. Sofia must learn that she could not profit from rumour and stolen, off-duty snaps. She knew nothing about him. He knew even less about her.

If Dom handled arrangements for the dinner correctly, that was how it would remain.

Sofia Acosta's rustic rural retreat, deep in the heart of Spain, where Sofia's brother Xander is tired of sitting for his portrait

'If you could stop painting for a moment and speak to me!' exclaimed the magnificent brute on his towering black stallion. 'I should never have agreed to this!'

'If you would stop ranting for a moment and keep still,' Sofia soothed, 'maybe I could finish this...'

Paintbrush high, she checked her work, and silently admitted that it was nigh on impossible to capture the darkly glittering glamour of a man who overshadowed everything in his immediate vicinity, including the stallion he was mounted on. 'Against all the odds,' she declared as she laid down her brush, 'I've finished. Come and see, if you like— I'm sure you'll love to see yourself blazing like a comet, fiercer than your stallion Thor.'

'Which is exactly the impression you intended to convey, I imagine,' Xander commented in a husky drawl as he eased his neck.

'Why must everything be sensational in your world, Sofia? Why can't you settle for calm?'

'If that's a reference to the article—' She stopped speaking as hurt overtook Sofia's natural desire to defend herself. Xander was her eldest brother, and the only one of the four prepared to listen to her defence when it came to an article that had appeared in print under her name but had been written by someone else. As of now she had nothing to back up her claim.

'You're a talented woman,' her brother insisted as he dismounted. 'You have your retreat, your riding… And you're a passable artist,' he remarked grudgingly as he scanned the canvas she'd been working on. 'You don't need to add journalist to your quiver of accomplishments. Be content with what you've got. Settle down. Enjoy life.'

'Like you?'

Xander ignored this reference to his continuing bachelor state. Having had responsibility for the entire family thrust upon him when their parents had died, he'd never loosened up and allowed himself to live.

'Why this pressing urge to see yourself in

print, Sofia? I'm guessing it must have paid well.'

That was what all her brothers thought—that she had sold her soul to the devil in return for a hefty pay-out. The truth was rather more complicated. She had never wanted to see her name in print, but the offer of lots of money to write 'something harmless' had proved irresistible. There were so many people she wanted to help at the retreat she had created. Without a constant flow of funds that was just impossible.

Since her mother's death, Sofia had lived her life as she believed her mother would have wanted her to, which included building a haven where others could escape for a while to recover from their difficult lives. Never in a million years had she imagined that once the article was written it would be changed, or that her brothers would be put under the same distorted spotlight.

Both they and Prince Cesar did so much good in the world, and yet some sleazy scribe had altered Sofia's words to make it seem that they and Cesar showed one face to the public, while living scandalous lives. If she didn't keep her mouth shut, there would be more articles, she had been promised, and these would be worse than the first. To protect her brothers she couldn't say anything, not even to Xander, though the article had done irreparable harm to their relationship.

Finding pony nuts in his pocket, Xander gave his stallion some treats before handing him over to a waiting groom. Turning around, he dipped his head to confront Sofia. 'Who wants to read everything in the garden of the super-rich is rosy? Was that your thinking? I don't understand you Sofia. Why didn't you come to me for money, instead of selling your cross-eyed opinions to that scurrilous rag?'

Because the damage had been done. The article she had written in good faith had already been changed.

'If you need money so badly I'll make you a loan right now—'

'No. Please!' Xander was always ready to save the day, but she had to do this to prove the article was a lie. The threat of a second article appearing under her by-line, mentioning trumped-up charges involving financial shenanigans between Cesar and her brothers, was enough to secure Sofia's silence.

'There's something you aren't telling me,' Xander stated with certainty.

This was the moment she should tell him the truth, but from the moment they had been orphaned, Xander had taken all the responsibility on his shoulders. She had to sort this out. 'I'm not a child any longer. I appreciate everything you've done for me, as we all do, but you must let me stand on my own two feet.'

'Your stubbornness will be the end of you,' Xander snapped as they left the barn. 'I can't understand why you picked out Cesar for special mention. He's done more good than you know, and yet you appear to have gone out of your way to undermine him. You put a country at risk with a few thoughtless words, making out that Cesar is a playboy prince when nothing could be further from the truth. I expected better of you, Sofia.'

She expected better of herself and, knowing she deserved every stinging word, she remained mute.

'Cesar would never discuss the good he

does,' Xander continued, frowning, 'and I've no doubt some of the readers will believe your piece of smut. The way you dwelled on him, anyone would think you were half in love with him and jealous of the life he leads.'

'Which only shows how little you know me.' She sounded defiant, but she was broken inside. Xander thinking so little of her hurt like hell. The article had paid well, and every penny of the money had gone to her retreat. The demand for places had expanded so rapidly she'd desperately needed additional funds. Naively believing that what she wrote would be printed word for word, the chance to write an article for a national newspaper had seemed too good to be true. And guess what?

As for falling in love with Cesar... The little she'd seen of that magnificent monster had convinced her that she could never fall in love with such a hard-bitten individual. She'd tried love and had found it a pallid substitute for the romantic novels that had informed her teenage years. That had been when she had been unable to secure a date. Having four high-octane brothers, overlooking her every move, had hardly been an incentive for likely suitors. Rubbing paint-covered hands down her paint-covered, overall, she took Xander to task on the subject of Cesar. 'Every single time I've met the man he's seemed insufferably superior.'

'I think you're harking back to one time when I had to remind you to curtsey when Prince Cesar visited our family home to trial some ponies. You were sixteen years old. Cesar was twenty-four. You may have noticed that over the years that he's changed. You've both changed. He's a hard man because he's had to be.'

Cesar had almost had the throne snatched from under his nose, she remembered. According to the press, a self-seeking man who cared nothing for the Queen, her family or the country had somehow weaselled his way into court, where, with a great deal of flattery and false promises, he had set about making himself indispensable to the Queen—a polite way of reporting he had been her lover. Having uncovered the truth and banished the conman from the kingdom, Cesar had stayed on at court to support and comfort his mother.

Sofia heaved a sigh. So he wasn't all bad, just autocratic, aloof and way beyond her reach.

'You will accept the Prince's invitation,' Xander stated firmly. 'His banquet will be your first step towards rehabilitation before you appear in the match.' She had to drag her mind back to the present as Xander continued, 'It's the least you can do. If the public sees you playing polo with the Prince, it will reassure them that things are back to normal.'

Whether it did or not, the thought of seeing Cesar again both chilled and excited her. As compelling as a human cyclone sweeping along on a wave of testosterone, Prince Cesar of Ardente was perfect hero material for susceptible females, but Sofia was neither susceptible nor was she in the mood for trembling in awe at a royal prince's feet. There was nothing more tiresome, in Sofia's opinion, than a six-foot-plus titan lording it over her, as she, with four self-opinionated brothers, was well placed to judge.

'We will attend Cesar's banquet as a family.' Xander stated in a tone that brooked no argument. 'He has requested a meeting with all of us, including his sister Olivia, after the banquet to discuss the upcoming charity polo matches, in which, I presume, you'll be playing.'

'Of course.' Sofia's retreat was one of the charities that would benefit. She could hardly refuse. Neither would she refuse the invitation to Cesar's banquet, though it meant confronting the man she had supposedly slammed in print. That was the best reason for attending she could think of. She'd see her brothers again, and if Cesar really thought so little of her, she had no further to fall.

CHAPTER TWO

HIS STAFF HAD outdone themselves. Never could he remember such a glittering scene. The dining table at his *palazzo* in Rome seated more than a hundred and each high-backed seat, sumptuously covered in night-blue velvet, was occupied tonight. Chandeliers sparkled like diamonds overhead, bouncing light off the jewels of those bound by wealth, power, pedigree, as well as an abiding passion for horses and polo. He was the only mongrel in the room.

His father's son by his mother's handmaid, Cesar had the Queen to thank for raising him as her own. She had plucked him from an un-certain future when Cesar's birth mother had abandoned him in favour of her latest lover. Romano born, he would now be Romano bred, the Queen had decreed. Though as soon as he was old enough to understand the im-plications of becoming heir to the throne, the

Queen had insisted that Cesar must curb his wild streak. She was still working on that.

'Is everything to your liking, sir?' his equerry asked.

'I can't thank you enough, Dom. Please convey my appreciation to the staff.'

Staring through the forest of crystal and silver ablaze like fire on a ground of white damask, his attention fixed on one woman. Sofia Acosta seemed confident and happy and was certainly animated as she chatted easily to his sister Olivia and to his mother, the Queen. His plan to spike Sofia's journalistic guns by seating her with the two women in the room who were strongest and most loyal to him appeared to be foundering. They were clearly enjoying each other's company.

He couldn't have seated Sofia Acosta far enough away, he reluctantly accepted. Even in another room, she would claim his interest. Cesar wasn't the only man present to have noticed the most fascinating woman in the room. What made Sofia so intriguing was the way she chatted so easily with his mother, and achieved what he would have believed impossible at a formal banquet, which was to make his mother laugh.

'You seem distracted.'

Sofia's brother Xander was seated next to him.

'My sister has not done something else to upset you tonight, I hope?' Xander suggested with concern.

'I've moved past that article, and we avoid each other whenever possible.' He hadn't spoken more than a curt hello to Sofia since she'd arrived at the *palazzo*.

'How will this distance between you work when you're playing in the same mixed polo team?'

'The match is in aid of charity. We'll forget our differences and concentrate on that.'

'That's very generous of you,' Xander commented. 'I'm not sure I could be quite so understanding.'

They shared a look. Both men were warriors; neither was understanding.

Cesar shrugged. 'Sofia's your sister and you are my close friend. I won't sully our friendship by carrying on a public feud with your sister.'

Xander raised an amused black brow. 'And this distance you talk of will be enough for you?'

'There's the entire length of a table between us tonight. And when we play our matches, the length of a polo mallet will suffice.'

'Just don't hurt her—emotionally hurt her, I mean. Sofia acts tough but she's always ready to be hurt, and that makes her vulnerable.'

'What do you take me for? I've no interest in her in that respect.'

'Don't you?'

Beyond the fact that Sofia would play an important part in the matches, no, of course he didn't. Who was he trying to kid? Cesar asked himself grimly as Sofia, together with his mother and his sister, threw back their heads and laughed.

How had she won them over so easily? He recalled his mother saying that royal life could be much improved if only people had the courage to express an honest opinion. He imagined Sofia had no trouble doing that. It had become obvious to him tonight that she was a natural communicator. But was she also a natural snoop, using this occasion to fuel another article?

The way to his mother's heart had always been unconventional. Sofia personified quirky with her abundant black hair cascading down her back in a shimmering waterfall of natural waves. Some attempt to tame it had been made. She'd tied a band of brightly coloured flowers around her forehead. Who did that at a royal banquet? He had to admit that the coronet of fresh blooms teamed perfectly with the summery, ankle-length gown Sofia had chosen to wear. With its intricate embroidery, jingling trinkets and happy, summer colours of yellow and pink, the dress perfectly mirrored the smile on her face.

A mix of anger and lust flashed through him. Sofia had the brass neck not only to outshine every other woman present but to sit amongst his guests as calm as you like. She'd clearly charmed the two people in the world who mattered most to him. Of course, his mother was notoriously tender-hearted, a thought that led him to study Sofia again. Was she as amusing and straightforward as she appeared tonight, or was Sofia Acosta a wolf in a rather attractive sheep's clothing?

Decision made, he excused himself from the table. Sofia exclaimed with surprise when he reached her chair. Bowing to his mother, the Queen, he dipped his head to murmur in Sofia's ear, 'I need you to come with me right now.'

Her eyes turned wide and curious. 'Are you throwing me out?' A smile was hovering around her mouth.

'Just come with me, please.'

They had attracted the attention of his mother. He smiled quickly for her sake.

'Is it time for pudding?' Sofia addressed herself to the Queen. 'Do we have to change places?'

His mother was laughed warmly. 'No, we do not change places between courses here.' She spared a sharp look at him. 'I believe my son would like to speak to you alone. Am I right, Cesar?'

'Correct,' he rapped, though his mother had managed to make it sound like a romantic assignation when nothing could be further from the truth. He was determined to address the issues between him and Sofia before the business of the meeting began.

He caught a whiff of some delicate wild-flower scent as Sofia left the table. With a pretty curtsey for his mother, she thanked the Queen for a wonderful evening.

'Come back to us,' his mother said, with a warning look to him.

'Don't we have a meeting after dinner with Sofia and her brothers?' his sister Olivia drawled with a knowing smile in his direction. Olivia was taunting him with the fact that, as she very well knew, more lay behind his desire to take Sofia from the table than business.

'Don't let us keep you, Sofia,' she added silkily. 'My brother appears to have something pressing on his mind.'

As well as on the placket of his evening trousers, he grimly recorded.

'A stroll in the garden?' he gritted out as soon as he and Sofia were out of earshot.

'You make it sound so appealing,' she murmured.

'Fresh air, and a chance to relive old times,' he proposed.

After what she'd done, he expected Sofia to at least have the good grace to pale at his challenge, but instead she firmed her jaw, inviting, 'Lead the way.'

'Life is more exciting when you say yes,' he remarked with irony.

'In some instances,' she countered.

'In all,' he insisted, striding on.

It was his eyes that made him irresistible, she decided as Cesar led her through the open glass doors and into the garden. Well, almost. *She* would resist, of course. Black sable in colour, they delivered a message no woman in charge of her senses could misinterpret. He had a particular mix of intensity and easy confidence that held the promise of sensational sex.

Brutally handsome, Cesar was savage on the polo field, which was why her brothers often fielded him on their team. And even before the infamous article the media had hinted at Cesar's extraordinary prowess in bed. Did every palace bedroom have a reporter sitting on the windowsill? Were there paparazzi in the bushes even now? she wondered as he led her deeper into the black, fragrant night.

What did Cesar want with her? Why was she here? Where sex was concerned, he was betting on a loser. She might be twenty-four, but her experience to date was incredibly limited, involving inept fumbles in a car, several lunges in the stable, subjecting her to an assortment of acne, halitosis, sloppy kisses and inept, searching hands. This was hardly the stuff of which dreams were made, and was definitely not sufficient preparation for a night-time encounter with Cesar.

'*Sprigati!*' Cesar urged as her footsteps lagged. 'Hurry up, Sofia!'

This was no romance, only impatience in his voice. So what was this about? Did he plan to rant about the article? He should. She deserved it. He'd probably warn her off ever writing about him again. She could handle that. She hadn't wanted to write about him in the first place.

'It's private enough here,' she stated firmly, refusing to take another step.

'Not private enough for me,' Cesar informed her curtly.

She sucked in an involuntary breath as he swung around to stare at her. Formidable by moonlight, and backlit by flickering torches, Cesar was an awesome sight. Sweet-smelling jonquil and delicate sprays of white star jasmine scrambling up a nearby wall, threatened to weaken her with their scent. Lifting her chin, she confronted him. Entirely by chance, she'd chosen the most romantic spot to stand her ground. Far beyond the palace walls the lights of the city provided a fitting backdrop for a man whose darkly glittering glamour rivalled even that of night-lit Rome.

Cesar's response was the lift of a brow. 'Well? Why have you stopped here?'

'I would like to know the purpose of this meeting.'

A humourless huff was her answer. 'You'll find out,' he called over his shoulder.

'Life is more exciting when you say yes.' Cesar's words banged in her brain. But what had she said yes to?

What was this woman doing to him? He could take his pick. Countless beauties vied for his attention. He wanted none of them because they were obvious and Sofia was not. She simmered with sexuality, yet retreated if he so much as looked at her a beat too long. Was she a virgin? Was that even possible at Sofia's age? Remembering her brothers, he thought it more likely than not. Which rubbished his thoughts on seducing her. The idea of bedding an innocent was inconceivable to him. He preferred older, more experienced women who knew the score, women who used him as he used them, for casual pleasure with no strings attached. His dealings with Sofia Acosta would, from this moment on, be solely restricted to business.

Things did not go entirely according to plan. Having led Sofia into a secluded, lamp-lit pavilion where they would be quite alone until the meeting with Sofia, his sister and her brothers began, she was immediately on guard. Angry and affronted as he was by what she'd done, he had no intention of terrorising her. To this end, he switched on the light and left the route to the door clear, while Sofia stood in the centre of the pavilion, staring at him with a multitude of questions in her eyes.

'What do you want of me, Cesar?'

He kept his distance, but her intoxicating scent had joined them by some invisible alchemy. Bringing the article to mind, he dismissed the magic with a cutting gesture of his hand. 'An explanation would be a start.'

'I'm so sorry, it was—'

'A mistake?' he queried, finding he couldn't contain his anger. 'A mistake that threatens to damage my reputation and that of your brothers?'

'How many times can I apologise?'

'I'm listening.'

'It wasn't what you think—'

'So it wasn't an appalling exposé?' When she didn't answer, he lost it completely. 'If you accepted my invitation to attend the banquet tonight so you could carry on "snooping" for another article, let me warn you that my legal team will take the newspaper down, and you with it.'

There was silence for a moment, only broken by the sound of the Acosta brothers laughing and joking as they approached. For a moment he saw surprise, even anger in Sofia's eyes, as if she'd forgotten the purpose

of the meeting, and perhaps thought he'd or-
chestrated a confrontation with her brothers
to get to the bottom of her reasons for writing the article.

Frowning, she confirmed these thoughts.
'I thought our meeting with my brothers and
your sister Olivia was scheduled to start after
the banquet?'

'It is,' he agreed. 'Can't you hear the orchestra? The dancing has already started.'

They stared at each other while electricity
between them sparked like a living force. It
was a force that would find no outlet tonight.

'You could help put out the agendas,' he
suggested. 'Clipboards? Now?' he proposed
when she continued to stare at him in bemuse-
ment. 'The charity matches?' he prompted.
She lifted her chin with an expression so like
his sister Olivia's he could have laughed. The
two women shared many characteristics—
combat being only one of them. Excellent.
He loved a good fight. 'Well? What are you
waiting for?'

'For you to say "please",' she suggested
mildly.

'*Please* sort out the clipboards,' he ground out, to end the impasse.

Gathering up half of them, she thrust them into his hands. 'Two work faster than one,' she explained, braving his astonished glance coolly. 'Shall I pull these tables around so we can face each other at the meeting?'

He could think of nothing he'd like less than to sit facing Sofia Acosta. Concentrating on anything else would prove impossible. 'This is an informal gathering when friends, who are also teammates, can snatch time in their busy schedules to discuss our upcoming matches.'

'We need clipboards for that?' she queried.

'Are you going to question every decision I make?'

'Only if I think it necessary.'

That level stare into his eyes again, and yet she seemed so calm and logical. The urge to see her wild with lust would have to keep for another time.

'My schedule is cast in stone,' he intoned icily. 'I've laid out an agenda so there can be no unnecessary mistakes in dates or overlaps in commitments.'

She pulled a wry face. 'I'm sure my brothers will love that.'

'I've already checked to make sure our schedules are in synchrony, and they agree with my plans.' Why was he even telling her this? he wondered as a brief wistful look swept over her features. Of course, since the article, he was closer to her brothers than she was. Was that his fault too?

'I'm glad my brothers are happy,' she said at last, with obvious sincerity, 'but does that mean anyone involved in the matches must sacrifice previous appointments to accommodate you?'

'Are you're talking about yourself?'

Her face paled but her lips firmed. 'I was thinking about your sister.'

'Ah, Olivia.' He huffed an ironic laugh. 'She wouldn't allow anything to stand in the way of riding with your brothers. As for you...'

'Yes?' Sofia's eyes narrowed in unmistakable challenge.

'I imagine you'd do anything to heal the rift you've created in your family.'

Perhaps that was a little harsher than he'd intended.

Sofia lowered her gaze but rallied fast. 'I'll study your agenda and let you know.'

As he quirked a brow, she queried, 'Men rule and women obey in your world?'

'You've met my mother and sister. Do you think that possible in my family? But playing in a team is different. Someone has to be in charge or chaos will ensue.'

'And that someone is you?' she challenged. 'Sounds as if you mean to be more dictator than team leader.'

Right on cue, his friends and fellow players, the Acosta brothers and his sister Olivia, came into sight in arrow formation, with Xander spearheading the group.

'I look forward to hearing your explanation of why you felt it necessary to cause such trouble with that article,' he told Sofia before they arrived, leaving her in no doubt that it hadn't been forgotten but had merely been postponed.

CHAPTER THREE

THE CHANCE TO ride with Cesar and her brothers was a lure Sofia would always find impossible to resist. How much more so under present circumstances? Having brothers breathing over her shoulder used to annoy her, but now she missed the closeness more than she could say. The change in their relationship since the article seemed irreparable sometimes, and determination alone wouldn't heal that rift.

She had to find a way to make her brothers believe her, but without being able to tell them everything for fear of them hitting out at Howard Blake, and him hitting out even harder, she was uncharacteristically powerless. Loyal to a fault, her brothers would see the false rant printed in the newspaper about Cesar, with Sofia's by-line proudly displayed at the top, as a blow against all of them.

In trying to save her retreat, she had only

succeeded in alienating those she loved most. The upcoming matches were the best chance she'd get to ride with her brothers on neutral territory. She hoped the physical demand of the matches would help to restore at least some of the camaraderie between them.

Her feelings where Cesar was concerned were conflicted. She was a moth drawn his very fierce flame. Cesar was shrewd, sexy and keenly intelligent. His body kept her awake at night. Dreams were safe. Reality was far more complicated. If she were foolish to offer herself up, as a waiter might offer a canapé, Cesar would swallow her down, lick his lips and move on. Leaving her where, exactly?

Embarking on a voyage of sensual discovery with Cesar would be like casting a minnow into a shark pool. She'd be saved that embarrassment as he couldn't have made it clearer in the pavilion, before her brothers and Olivia arrived, that he would never forgive her for what she'd done.

As the meeting went on, Cesar didn't attempt to include her in the discussion, while her brothers gave her thin smiles when they looked at her at all. Only Olivia pressed her lips together in a reassuring smile, as if she, at least, wanted to believe better of Sofia.

'Are we done here?'

She jumped to attention as Olivia spoke.

'I have a rendezvous later,' the Princess revealed.

'A *rendezvous*?' Cesar demanded icily. 'With whom, exactly?'

'A friend.' That was as much as Olivia was prepared to divulge. This seemed to amuse Sofia's brothers, though for the sake of Cesar they confined their feelings to sideways glances. What were they hiding now? she wondered.

She didn't have to wait long to find out.

Xander was as heated as Cesar when it came to issuing instructions. 'Make sure you're never on your own. Don't do anything that might put you at risk.'

'Isn't that rather the point of a rendezvous?' Olivia drawled with amusement, sliding a conspiratorial glance Sofia's way.

This was one situation she didn't want any part of. Breaking the stand-off, she moved to the door. 'I should get back to my room to log all these dates in my calendar.'

'We can walk back together,' Olivia agreed, seeming as keen as Sofia to escape the mounting tension.

When five autocratic individuals thought they could manipulate the lives of two young women, they had another think coming. Both Sofia and Olivia had endured brotherly smothering as children, and neither of them was prepared to roll over and accept a command simply because one of the titans had uttered it.

'Not so fast.'

She stared at Cesar's hand on her arm.

'We haven't finished talking,' he informed her.

She moved away from the doorway to allow everyone else to leave. 'What do you want to talk about?'

'I think you know,' he insisted. 'You speak and I listen.'

'And then you judge me?' She was trembling inwardly, but that was something he didn't need to know. Could anyone be more attractive, while appearing so hard and autocratic, than Cesar Romano? Cesar was as huggable as an iceberg, and as distant as a faraway sun. 'In my world conversation flows back and forth.'

His stern expression didn't change by as much as a flicker. 'I will evaluate your excuses when I've heard them.'

'So I'm already guilty in your eyes?'

'I have the evidence in print.' He said this with an easy shrug. 'If you can have something that might reverse my conclusion that you are a cold-blooded, money-grabbing traitor to your kind, then please let me know.'

'My *kind*?' she repeated tensely. 'Do you think I imagine myself as lofty as you?'

'I have no idea what you think, but I do know I find it hard, if not impossible, to contemplate working with you on the team unless I have some understanding of what drove you to be so condemning in print. In case you're in any doubt, the only reason you're on the team is because of your prowess as a rider, and the attention your notoriety will bring to the match.'

She had no excuses to offer. Desperate to raise money for her retreat, she'd been tasked with providing details of life behind the glamorous polo scene, little realising she was going to be manipulated by a newspaper mogul called Howard Blake. There was no point now in wishing she hadn't taken that call. She'd been naïve, thinking the polo scene, with its royal connections and appeal to various celebrities, would be something people wanted to read about. She hadn't realised that in writing a harmless article she had inadvertently provided Blake with enough detail to flesh out, making his lies seem perfectly believable.

Now she wondered if Cesar had been his target all along. Prince Cesar certainly had the most to lose when it came to reputational damage. Her brothers could shrug it off. Though that wasn't what they'd told Sofia, of course. In truth, any attempt to tarnish their reputation only enhanced it, for with the exception of Dante, who was now a happily married man, her brothers prided themselves in being the bad boys of polo.

'What?' Cesar pressed, jolting her out of her reveries. 'Not a word of explanation?'

None that she could tell Cesar. First she

must find a way to curb Howard Blake's bullying ways. His next victim might be more vulnerable than she was. Blake had already threatened to bring down her brothers if she went public with the fact that he'd changed her words and, goodness knew, there was enough rumour and scandal to damn them. With Sofia's relationship with her brothers already stretched to the limit, she couldn't risk it taking another blow.

'I have no excuse,' she said flatly. 'The invitation to write the article came at a time when I needed money badly, so I wrote a story I knew would sell.'

'*You* needed money?' Cesar demanded with incredulity, no doubt thinking about her brothers' massive combined wealth.

'I have no part in my brothers' tech empire. I launched the retreat with my own money. It grew to a point where I needed a much wider-ranging roster of staff, and that requires proper funding.'

'You couldn't ask your brothers for money?' Cesar exclaimed with disbelief.

'Of course not. I stand on my own two feet.'

'This one defamatory article will keep

your retreat running for how long?' His stare pierced her. Cesar's mind was already made up. She was guilty as charged.

'You don't know me, yet you set yourself up as my judge and jury and, if you had your way, executioner.'

Cesar's expression turned as black as thunder. 'And you only know what you've read about me,' he fired back.

She couldn't deny it.

'Gutter journalism,' he derided. 'Aren't you ashamed, coming from a family as proud and as upstanding as yours'?'

Cesar was viciously opposed to everything she stood for. She had to keep her nerve. She could so easily make things worse with careless words, and that would mean losing that closeness with her brothers for ever.

'I imagine you made a pretty penny out of the rubbish that was printed.'

'It wasn't *my* rubbish. It was heavily edited—'

'Rubbish,' Cesar supplied. 'It's easy to deny you had any part in it now.'

'Believe me or not, that's your prerogative.

I had no say in the finished article, and every penny I was paid went to support my retreat.'

Disbelief was written all over Cesar's face. 'I'm giving you a chance to clear your name,' he stated harshly. 'This may be your only chance. I suggest you think hard and long before you walk away from me tonight.'

'I don't think anything I say will make you change your mind, so I see no point in staying.'

'I'm sure not,' he agreed.

His short laugh chilled her. She glanced at the door. 'I should be getting back.'

'We both should. I will escort you. Far be it from me to see harm come to any woman, even you. I can only think you're a cuckoo in the family. Regardless of what you've done to them, I know your brothers would do anything to protect you, and I respect their wishes.'

A now familiar blaze of shame burned through Sofia's veins. But one thing was nagging. There had been detail in that finished article that even she hadn't known. So who had? She would have to find out to stand a chance of making peace with her brothers and Cesar.

'I thought you might have more pride,' Cesar remarked as they walked side by side through the gardens to the palace. He made it sound as if she'd disappointed him.

'I have no pride,' she said honestly. 'If I have to wash dishes to keep my retreat going, then that's what I'll do.'

'In between selling more stories on those you profess to help?' he bit out.

The calm she was fighting so hard to maintain was shattered. Trust was perhaps the most vital element in a sanctuary where people came to recover and rebuild their lives. The thought of disclosing even the smallest detail she'd been told by one of the guests was as shocking to Sofia as seeing her brothers and Cesar damned in print.

'At least you have the good sense to appear ashamed of your actions,' he commented as they slowed on their approach to the open doors to the banqueting hall.

Shame was the least of it. This was the first time that she had been faced by the fact that Howard Blake might target her retreat. He must be stopped, but to do that she'd need help. Powerful men like Cesar and her brothers were the only individuals she knew with sufficient clout to curb Blake's bullying, but the truth would have to come out.

Cesar gave her a brief sideways glance. 'You appear confused.'

'Not confused,' she assured him. Suddenly everything was crystal clear. 'I need your help,' she admitted.

'So you're every bit as self-seeking and as selfish as I thought? *You* cause the damage, and now *you* need help?'

She was determined not to show her feelings. Hiding how stung she felt had been second nature growing up. She'd soon learned not to blub in front of her brothers.

'I made a mistake,' she confessed. 'And now I want the chance to make things right.'

'Why don't you take some well-earned respite at your retreat?' he demanded sarcastically. Whirling on his heel, Cesar made to peel away. 'You can find your own way from here.'

She caught hold of his arm. 'Cesar, please...'

He didn't shake her off, and his expression

was calculating. The punch to her senses was extraordinary. 'Are you sure it's rehabilitation you're looking for? Or do you have something else in mind?'

She sucked in a sharp breath, but desire never came first for Sofia. She squashed her feelings to concentrate on others, but now she must forget her pride, forget about being a cool-headed woman, and just this once risk everything for the chance to make things right.

He couldn't have been more surprised when Sofia stood on tiptoe to brush a kiss against his lips. 'I'm sorry,' she whispered.

Feelings rampaged inside him at the realisation that Sofia wanted more than to apologise. He knew the signals. This was unusual play for a woman who had betrayed him, and betrayed her brothers, yet for all her bravado there were shadows behind her eyes, and that set up doubt regarding her guilt. He had to know more before he took things further.

Did he care enough to find out?

'Aren't you in enough trouble?' he demanded harshly. 'Go back to the ballroom.

There should be more than enough distractions there to keep you occupied.'

'Cesar, please...'

Tension swirled around them as she clutched his arm. Reluctantly, he admired her grit.

'I need to talk to you, Cesar, nothing else, I promise.'

He gave her a cynical look to find her eyes pleading and her lips tempting. He was no saint. She matched him like a tiger, kissing him fiercely as she thrust her body against his. It was as if some force beyond their control had taken them over, Sofia especially, until they were bound together in a dance as old as time.

But something was off kilter. Was desperation driving Sofia's passion or were her feelings for him genuine? Would he ever know? Concluding that deciphering her motives was beyond him right now, he pulled back.

'Did I do something wrong?' she asked, staring up with confusion in her eyes.

'You did nothing wrong.'

She had tasted of honey and innocence, so if anyone was at fault he was. Her mouth was swollen and red where his stubble had abraded it, and her eyes were bottomless pools of distress. *But was that an act too?*

'Why are you doing this?' she asked, rubbing the back of her hand across her mouth, as if to hide the evidence of how much each of them had invested in one single kiss. 'Why kiss me at all?' she demanded. 'Why not ignore me and wait for the evening to end? Then you wouldn't need to see me again until we ride in the matches.'

'I might ask you the same question,' he pointed out.

'You don't want this,' she said with sudden certainty, shaking her head. 'I forced myself on you.' Her face crumpled. 'How you must hate me.'

The idea of Sofia forcing herself on him made him want to laugh, but he couldn't be that cruel. 'Hate is a powerful word,' he commented mildly instead.

'But I can see fire burning in your eyes,' she claimed. 'So why kiss me, Cesar? *Why?*'

'I could say you started it.' He kept his hands loosely looped around Sofia's waist. She made no attempt to break free. 'And you kissed me back. So why did you do that?' he asked with genuine interest.

She was silent and then her eyes cleared as she admitted with faint surprise, 'I couldn't stop myself.'

Appearing seductive, as she most certainly did, yet vulnerable might be part of Sofia's script. She had caused more trouble than could be imagined. Proving he was worthy to rule was a lifelong task, and an article hinting at financial irregularities in his past, however fictitious, did him no favours. He'd embraced responsibility for his country gladly. His countrymen would always come first, and Sofia Acosta would not be allowed to distract him.

'Seems to me you were consumed by that same impulse to kiss me.' Growing embarrassment reddened her cheeks.

He shrugged off her suggestion. 'Everyone's entitled to a momentary lapse.'

'Even me?' she asked.

If he could forget all the doubts and half-truths and uncertainties currently swirling around them, Sofia was perfect, and he wanted her. His body was aroused to the point of pain, but it was the challenge in Sofia's eyes that made her irresistible. Her lustrous hair, tumbling in wild profusion to her waist, glinted like black diamonds in the muted light, making the temptation to fist a hank, so he could draw back her head to taste the soft skin of her neck, was overwhelming. But why give her that pleasure?

'Perhaps that stupid kiss was a lapse we should both accept and move on?' she suggested.

Sofia Acosta was beyond infuriating, yet he loved the way she could rally so fast and come back fighting. Her dark gaze brightened as she intuited his thoughts. Or was that a scheming light? Maybe her only reason for kissing him was to soften his mood in order to dig up more dirt to use in another article.

'Who are you, Sofia?' Holding her at arm's length, he dipped his head to stare into her eyes. 'I can't decide if you're a rogue member of the Acosta family, who cares nothing for your brothers' love or your family's reputation, or if you're under some form of duress?'

Was he imagining it, or did she flinch when

he said that? 'If there's something on your mind, please, tell me.'

He was so certain she was about to say something revealing, but Sofia's hesitation suggested she thought him as dangerous as whatever was causing the shadows behind her eyes. *Dios!* Would he never find out the truth about this woman?

There was only one certainty here, and that was the heat rising between them.

'Is this what you want?' he demanded.

'Yes!' she exclaimed, eyes closing, lips parting as his hand found her.

'Then I suggest you find someone else to ease your frustration. I don't play games with dangerous little girls.'

CHAPTER FOUR

CESAR STALKED BACK towards the palace, leaving Sofia standing on her own. She couldn't catch her breath, let alone order her thoughts. Kissing him had been a huge mistake that had left her feeling embarrassed and humiliated. Giving in to wild impulses would only ever lead to trouble. Judging by his expression, she couldn't have sunk any lower in Cesar's opinion.

Not only did he believe her to be a gutter journalist but someone who held her body cheaply, like a counter to be played when it suited her. What irony that nothing could be further from the truth. Her body might ache for Cesar's touch, but not like this, furtively and wildly, but passionately, truthfully and openly. With a long, shaking sigh she dragged herself back into the moment. It was vital to clear her head before returning to the party.

She found it easier than expected to remain

in the gardens, where the scent of blossom soothed her. It was quiet and removed from the upbeat atmosphere inside the brilliantly lit palace ballroom, which gave her chance to search her mind for a solution to keep her retreat afloat.

On top of that, she had to keep her brothers and Cesar and any future victims safe from a blackmailing tyrant. Cesar was the most obvious ally. No one wielded more power than he did, but she'd lost his trust. He couldn't have made it clearer that he despised what she'd done, and despised the person he believed she'd become. He wasn't alone in that. Right now she hated herself, but it was no use crying over spilt milk. She smoothed her hair. This was a time for action, not brooding. It would take too long to try to win back Cesar's trust by small increments. She had to be bold, and the only way she knew how to be bold was in the saddle.

The retreat she had created, on land left to her by her parents, was another gentle, contemplative setting, created specifically to house those who badly needed help to rebuild their lives. She could see now that her paintings had been her way of escaping reality, but what was needed going forward was Sofia in warrior mode. There could be no more missteps or hesitation. She had always looked out for herself, and her next task was to convince one of the most commanding men on earth to join forces and help her defeat a bully.

Well, that should be easy, Sofia reflected as she made her way back through the night-fragrant garden. Her body burned with arousal after the encounter with Cesar, while her mind was burning up with embarrassment. Cesar didn't trust her. He didn't like her. And though he needed her to ride in his charity polo matches, he almost certainly wouldn't shed a tear if he never saw her again. But since when had life been easy? There was always a new hurdle to jump. This one just happened to be higher than most.

Having studied Cesar's famous agenda, it was immediately clear that where anything was connected to him, money was no object. First-class travel arrangements had been made for all, including the horses. With influential contacts across the globe, Cesar naturally anticipated that everyone's path be as smooth as his. He could alter the destiny of a country at a stroke of his pen, for goodness' sake, and all she needed was for Cesar to help her end the bullying tactics of one wicked man.

First she'd have to win back his trust and change his opinion of her. The feat loomed ahead of her like an insurmountable wall.

Then it was a wall she'd go around, or go through, Sofia determined.

She paused before entering the ballroom to allow her heartbeat to steady. She would need every bit of her composure to confront Cesar again. Most important of all was to hide her feelings for him. Attraction had no part to play in this. She had a job to do.

Dannazione! Where had she gone? Where was Sofia? Had she fled the party? Gut instinct said no. Sofia wasn't the type to run away from anything or anyone. She'd had to be gutsy to survive four hard-living brothers—and him, Cesar reflected as he unconsciously swiped the back of his hand across his mouth where her lips had touched his.

Only one Acosta brother had found love. He

turned to look at the team's fitness trainer, Jess, whose husband was Dante Acosta. Jess was a down-to-earth farmer's daughter and a trained physiotherapist, who had helped to heal her husband when doctors had practically given up on Dante submitting to the months of treatment required. They somehow managed to combine Jess's career with Dante's business and polo-playing schedule, and quite obviously their love for each other was blooming, as Dante had confided that family life came first.

Dante had been lucky finding Jess, but lightning never struck the same place twice, and neither Cesar nor Sofia's other brothers had even come close to finding a soul mate.

'Cesar...'

Sofia! He swung round. 'I thought you might have left the party.'

'Is seeing me a good surprise or a bad one?' she asked coolly.

It was impossible not to notice how beautiful she was, and how appealing only she could be with a coronet of fresh flowers in her hair. 'What do you want?' he asked, impatient with himself for feeling this way about her.

'Bad surprise, I take it,' she said.

He frowned.

'I'm here to apologise,' she explained. 'There's no mileage in you and me being enemies. We have to work together during the charity polo matches so we can raise as much money we can. Why not declare peace now?'

He shot her a cynical look. Sofia had many things to apologise for, but he didn't feel inclined to drive her away. 'Why don't you find somewhere to sit and enjoy the party while you can?'

'While I can?' she queried. 'Do you expect something to go wrong imminently?'

Ignoring that, he offered to find her a seat. He scanned the crowded ballroom.

'I can find my own place to sit down,' she assured him, 'but thank you.'

'I could deliver you back to my mother.'

'Like a missing parcel?' she suggested, starting to smile.

He shrugged. 'It would be the polite thing to do.'

'In that case, I accept.'

But she trembled at his touch. Her expression, however, remained carefully neutral.

'You're too kind,' she told him when he brought her in front of the Queen.

'I'm not kind at all,' he murmured in Sofia's ear, 'and you would do well to remember that.'

Then his mother took over, smiling at their approach. 'Ah, Cesar, I was wondering how long it would be before you asked Sofia to dance.'

'Dance with Sofia?' He couldn't hide his surprise.

His mother glossed over his lapse in good manners by drawing Sofia forward to kiss her on both cheeks.

'You've been far too kind,' she told his mother.

'Nonsense,' his mother insisted. 'I notice Olivia is dancing with one of your brothers. Well, Cesar,' his mother pressed, 'why are you keeping Sofia waiting?'

Why indeed?

'If Cesar doesn't feel like dancing—' Sofia began to protest, clearly not keen to feel his arms around her.

'Nonsense. Of course he does,' his mother the Queen insisted in a tone he'd never heard her use before. 'How can my son refuse to dance with such a beautiful guest?' This query was accompanied by a long, hard stare at him.

Sofia slid him a withering look. This was no puling princess touting for a crown, or some celebrity social climber with vaunting ambition, but a real woman with genuine feelings and a history that he could never forget. Any interaction between them was bound to be tense and awkward.

'Cesar?' his mother prompted.

'I can refuse you nothing,' he told his mother sincerely.

'Good!' the Queen exclaimed. 'I shall increase my demands in future.'

'I have no doubt of that,' he murmured, exchanging an amused look with a woman he held in the very highest regard.

'Well?' she urged. 'What are you waiting for? I'm sure Sofia is longing to dance with her Prince.'

If looks could kill he would be dead. His mother, usually keenly observant, had missed the opposition to this idea on Sofia's face. 'This is no easier for me than it is for you,' he assured Sofia once they were out of earshot. 'One dance and then we're done.'

'Until the matches, when we'll be thrown together again,' she reminded him with a rueful slant of her mouth.

'When that happens, you'll do your job and I'll do mine,' he stated firmly.

'To the very best of my ability,' Sofia promised with a long, fearless look into his eyes.

He gave a cynical huff, but it was hard not to believe her. No one could accuse Sofia Acosta of entering into anything in half-measures. When they reached the edge of the dance floor, in deference to his rank the other couples stopped dancing and stood back. If he refused to dance with Sofia, there would be food for gossipmongers the world over. The orchestra struck up a waltz in keeping with their splendid surroundings.

'I've heard of dancing with the devil,' Sofia murmured dryly.

'Are we taking it one step further?' he suggested.

'The demon on horseback dancing with

the devil?' she remarked. 'At least we should march to the same beat.'

But they didn't march, they danced as closely as two people could. 'Relax,' he suggested. 'Unless you aim to cause comment.'

'More than I already have?' Sofia countered. 'Just by being here I've caused comment. No one has forgotten the article.'

'Including me,' he assured her, 'but I choose to rise above it, and this is a wonderful opportunity to stop the rumourmongers in their tracks.'

'Is that the only reason you agreed to dance with me?'

'Can you think of any other?'

Noticing how many people were covertly using their mobile phones to take pictures of them, he drew Sofia even closer. He might have expected her to pull away, but at least in that she had more sense. 'Let's play their game,' she said, surprising him.

'Why not?' he agreed, softening a little towards her as she smiled into his eyes.

Playing the game turned out to be more arousing than even he could have imagined. Who was dancing with the devil now? Devil

Woman was an apt description of the siren in his arms. Sofia managed to be both sensual and tasteful as she moved in time to the music, leaving no one in any doubt—apart from him—that they were completely reconciled. More couples joined them on the floor and were courteous enough to allow them a degree of privacy.

'When did you learn to be such a good actress?' he murmured, his mouth very close to her ear.

'Am I acting?'

It wasn't just her voice that trembled now, her body quivered against his like a doe at bay with a rutting stag in the immediate vicinity. 'I hope you are,' he dismissed, pressing home his advantage. 'I know I am.'

'And I thought you were a gentleman,' she told him in the softest, most pleasing voice, 'but now I know you're just a prince.'

'Ouch!' He barked a laugh at the punchline. 'Not all princes are the same, and please remember this is just for show.'

'Hmm, I noticed,' she commented.

Why was he surprised when she brushed

her body against his? Hadn't he touched Sofia intimately and left her hanging?

'Is this just an act?' she whispered, no doubt referring to his rapidly expanding erection.

'No act,' he assured her. 'You are an extremely provocative woman.'

Her black eyes sparkled with challenge. 'As you are an extremely provocative man. Shall we keep on dancing, or cause comment by standing here in the middle of the floor?'

Couples were revolving around them like spokes around the hub of a wheel. 'Forgive me,' he said dryly. 'I had quite forgotten the need to dance.'

'*I* distracted you?' she asked with a sceptical lift of one brow.

'You…surprise me,' was the most he was prepared to admit.

'So you're allowed to touch, but I'm not?'

'You must follow your instinct,' he advised as they swirled in time to the ironically carefree strains of a Viennese waltz.

'That might get me into trouble,' she said, pushing her lips down as if that didn't worry her too much.

'Past experience suggests you can handle

it,' he countered, 'though I've noticed that you can say one thing while your body responds quite differently. I'd love to know what's really going on in your head.'

'Like you, I'm trying to give the impression that everything is rosy between us,' she assured him. 'There's nothing to be gained by the charities we support if rumour suggests we're at each other's throats.'

'Friction between us might draw even more crowds,' he observed.

'Better to leave your guests with an air of mystery, to add intrigue to what they've seen tonight, don't you think?' she asked as phones were pointed in their direction.

The fact they fitted together perfectly was enough for him for now. Sofia's clean wildflower scent beguiled his senses, while her hair felt like silk as it brushed against the hand he had lodged in the small of her back. Her breath was a cool, minty draught that made the urge to plunder her mouth rise like madness inside him—which would be a sensation too far for his guests. As a man gossip didn't faze him, but as a prince he was forced to curb his natural instincts. It was enough to give the impression that all was well between him and Sofia, so as far as onlookers were concerned he had forgiven her and all was well.

'Don't you like the music?' Sofia probed as they danced on.

'Why do you say that?'

'You seem preoccupied.'

Remembering to smile for the sake of the watching guests, he conceded, 'I am preoccupied.'

'Is it anything I can help with? Have I made things awkward for you?' she added as he huffed a short laugh.

'You?' he queried.

'Okay, I get it. This is an act, and you'd prefer it if I said nothing at all.'

'No. Please speak,' he encouraged. 'Conversation between us will reinforce the impression that we like each other.'

'When nothing could be further from the truth?' she suggested.

He knew better than to answer that. 'Don't overdo it,' he warned as Sofia gave a cynical laugh. 'A happy expression on your face is enough, though you could try to relax a little more.'

'You make that so easy,' she responded sarcastically as the orchestra segued into another popular Viennese melody. 'At least the conductor thinks you're enjoying yourself.'

'My master of music can't be expected to read my mind.'

They danced on until a question occurred to him. 'Do you have enough material for your next article?'

Forgetting the act they were supposed to be playing, Sofia pulled back with a gasp of surprise. 'I'm here because you invited me to the party.'

'A necessary evil to avoid offending your brothers,' he said bluntly.

'How gracious you are,' she murmured beneath her breath, growing stiff and unyielding in his arms.

He was pleased to see she managed to smile, as if there was nothing she would rather be doing than dancing with him. Sensibly, he maintained a distance between them, and throughout the dance there was an expression of enjoyment on his face. It wasn't all hard work. Forced to bring Sofia close in order to avoid collisions on a packed dance floor meant intimate contact with the soft contours of her body was inevitable.

Sofia was a good dancer. Fit and supple, she moved instinctively to the music. The gown she had chosen to wear was of such a fine fabric it did little to conceal her form. Her hand was tiny in his, but her grip was firm. He had one hand lodged in the small of her back so he could feel her trembling. Careful not to adjust his fingers by as much as a millimetre, he took her around the floor. There would be no subtle messages between him and Sofia tonight.

'That must have been torture for you,' she observed when they finally stopped dancing.

'I've known worse.'

'Will you join me in the garden?' she surprised him by asking as they approached the French doors.

She was looking across the room to where guests were spilling out onto the balcony to enjoy the still balmy evening. The romantic setting in a lovely garden, beneath a black velvet sky peppered with stars and lit by the light of a silvery moon, was surely unparalleled. And would therefore be completely wasted on a couple like them. 'Why?' he asked suspiciously.

'Why not?' she countered. 'How are we supposed to become effective team members if you and I remain at daggers drawn? And,' she added, glancing around, 'people are still watching us, and I think that walking outside for a breath of fresh air after dancing is the most natural thing to do.'

She was right in that a fragrant breeze was drifting in from the gardens, but he'd done his duty and felt no urge to do more.

'Please,' Sofia whispered, putting a hand on his arm. 'I'd like the chance to start making things right between us.'

'Another new approach?' he suggested cynically.

Her cheeks flushed red, as she no doubt remembered them kissing earlier. 'It's important to break this deadlock between us,' she insisted. 'We're going to be working together.'

'To heal that gulf would take more than a moonlit stroll,' he informed her, and with a curt bow he left Sofia to enter the garden on her own.

CHAPTER FIVE

SHE MIGHT HAVE known Cesar would reject her olive branch. He'd made up his mind that she was guilty. Dancing together had been nothing but a necessary evil, as far as the Prince was concerned. While for her it had been thrilling. At least his guests had seemed convinced the trouble between them was over. Wasn't that all that mattered?

Apart from the fact that he had left every part of her tingling with the memory of his touch?

She had the rest of the evening to fret over going too far. Trust took time to establish, and she'd waded in with her hobnailed boots. And was so quickly lost, she reflected with a glance at her brothers. The rift between them made her desperately sad. The article had done more harm than she could mend in a single night, and she longed to make things right.

That opportunity might come at Cesar's training camp, which was where they were heading next. She might have felt more confident about that if Cesar hadn't ignored her for the rest of the evening. Deciding to sleep on the problem, she took her leave of the Queen and kissed Princess Olivia on both cheeks. She was fast coming to see Olivia as a kindred spirit.

'Sleep well, my dear,' the Queen said kindly. 'And, please, don't be a stranger.'

As they exchanged warm glances Sofia found it hard to imagine that such a poised and beautiful woman as the Queen could fall into the clutches of a conman. According to the press, that was exactly what had happened. Stricken by grief after the death of her husband, Queen Julia had searched for company online, but what had appeared to be the concern of a handsome stranger had turned out to be nothing more than a wicked plot to seize the throne. Evil always seemed to strike when a victim was at their lowest ebb. Sofia felt a great wave of sympathy wash over her as she said goodnight to the Queen.

'And remember,' Olivia said as Sofia turned to go, 'if you're still hungry Cesar's kitchens are open twenty-four seven to accommodate his huge appetite.'

Sofia didn't want to consider Cesar's appetite, huge or otherwise, but she thanked the Princess warmly, and felt lighter at the thought that the seeds of friendship really were growing between them.

First she went to her sumptuous suite of rooms to draw a great steadying breath. The suite overlooked a lake beyond the palace gardens, and had been designed to imbue a guest with a feeling of relaxation.

Most guests, Sofia's reflected. Her mind was churning with unanswered questions. And that made her hungry. Untying the laces on her dress, she allowed the glorious fabric to drift to the floor. Seeing herself in the free-standing mirror in just a flimsy thong and bra, with her hair flowing free and a coronet of fresh flowers on her head, she decided with a wry smile that she was only short of a waterfall to act the part of water nymph, with perhaps a rugged stranger riding by—

one who felt compelled to rein in his horse to take a closer look.

Quickly followed by a team of brothers with towels and sarcastic remarks.

So much for daydreams!

She took a quick shower and then changed into jeans and a casual top before exploring downstairs in the hope of finding the kitchen. Guests were milling about when she came down the sweeping mahogany staircase. No one would be in a hurry to bring such a successful evening to a close, she guessed as the orchestra struck up a fresh tune.

There would be snacks at dawn, her brothers had informed her with relish. Big men with big appetites, goodness knew where her brothers were now. Cesar's *palazzo* had become a hotbed of passion, judging by the number of couples entwined in the shadows of the great hall. Not for this Acosta, Sofia reflected wryly as she followed a waiter through some grand double doors. She was hungry for food and nothing more.

Until she saw Cesar, stripped off to a pair of jogging pants and a form-fitting top, with his wild black hair only partially tamed by a red bandana.

'The party over for you too,' he said as he took a bite out of a king-sized burger. 'Hungry?' he enquired.

'What about your guests?' she asked, speaking on autopilot while she tried to get over the shock of seeing him dressed down and casual while the elegant party was still in full swing.

'It's the host's prerogative to take a break if he wants.' His shoulders eased in a careless shrug. 'My guests can join me down here if they like, though I doubt they're missing me. Burger smell good?' he said as she stared at him. 'I can recommend it.'

'Coming right up,' the young chef on duty offered with a smile.

'I don't want to put you to any trouble,' Sofia insisted.

'No trouble,' the young man insisted. 'Onions?'

'When in Rome...' She glanced at Cesar.

'I think she's saying, yes, please,' Cesar interrupted.

'Sorry. Yes, please,' she echoed, with an apologetic grin for the chef.

Cesar remained lounging back against the wall. 'Are you sure you don't mind my being here?' This was his *palazzo*, his kitchen, his chef.

'Be my guest,' he invited. 'But I forgot,' he added, 'you are my guest.'

'And most grateful for your hospitality.'

'Don't overdo it, Sofia,' Cesar warned with dry amusement.

Making peace with this man wouldn't be easy, but when had she ever embraced easy?

'Take the rest of the night off,' Cesar told the chef. 'Others can take your place. You've put in some long hours today. I appreciate it,' he added as the young chef handed over Sofia's burger.

'That was nice of you,' she commented as they munched.

'You could try not to sound quite so surprised.'

'You're as bad as my brothers!' she exclaimed as Cesar stole the rest of her bun from her plate.

'Worse,' he assured her.

She hummed agreement. 'I remember a time when you were imperious.'

'Never with my staff, though I do remember one incident when I had to deal with an infuriating tomboy on an *estancia* deep in Spain.'

Her jaw dropped. 'So you admit it?'

'On that one occasion? Yes. You were a pest.'

'And you were an imperious prince, taking up space in my stable.'

'You never had a sense of what was good for you.'

'Maybe because what's good for me has never been uppermost in my mind.'

'Does that bring us back to the article?' Cesar suggested with a long sideways look.

She sighed. 'That was a mistake. I should have known. I'm no good being at anything but what I am.'

'Clearly,' Cesar agreed. 'Though there's not much you're afraid of, is there?'

Wrong. She was desperately afraid of losing her brothers' trust, and her own self-belief, if she couldn't clear her name. Losing Cesar's regard would be yet another blow.

'Let's take that stroll in the garden,' he said

when they'd rinsed their hands and cleared their plates away.

This was a pivotal moment when her life could change for better or worse, but at least they were talking.

Inviting Sofia into the garden only proved that damping down his feelings where Signorina Acosta was concerned wasn't as easy as he had supposed. He should refuse to have anything more to do with her, but like a wood nymph beckoning him ever deeper into the thicket of her life Sofia was irresistible.

When he'd suggested the walk, Sofia's surprise had betrayed the fact that she hadn't believed he'd want to spend time with her. When her gaze darkened and her cheeks flushed pink, he knew her answer would be yes. The electricity was sparking between them again. He'd worked out in the gym then showered and changed after leaving the banquet, with Sofia a constant in his mind.

And now, with her long hair still damp from the shower, and silky corkscrews of baby hair arranged like a filmy crown around her brow, she was beautiful. She'd washed off her make-up but not the smudge of chocolate on her neck. The urge to lick it off was overwhelming.

'Snacking on treats in your bedroom?' he guessed. In area, at least, she found temptation irresistible. All his guests were supplied with everything they might need, including ingredients for a midnight feast.

'How do you know?' she demanded, frowning.

'Elementary, my dear Watson. You have chocolate on your neck.'

She relaxed enough to smile. 'Aren't you concerned that your guests might see you in the garden dressed like this, and wonder what you're up to in the garden with me?'

'My guests have everything they could possibly need, and I'm sure they're quite capable of amusing themselves without my assistance.'

'I'm sure they are,' she agreed, 'but—'

'But what?' he interrupted. 'Don't you trust yourself alone with me in the garden?'

She hummed and gave him a look.

'You find me irresistible?' he proposed.

'Do I?'

'Don't worry, I'll keep a tight rein on you.'

'That might work,' she agreed huskily, on what sounded like a dry throat.

'As you so rightly say,' he pointed out as they moved off, 'we're going to be together, so we might as well clear the air.'

Was there anywhere on earth more beautiful than Cesar's Roman garden? Lit by moonlight, marble statues stood in silent repose like elegant ghosts from ancient times that at any moment might step down from their pedestals to join them. Beyond the vast expanse of garden the lights of Rome sparkled like precious gems. Floral fragrances teased her senses, lending a soothing quality to the setting they had chosen to have this talk that was at odds with the tension between them. But when a band was stretched tight it had to snap at some point. She was acutely aware of Cesar at her side. For some reason, she was drawn to the now deserted pavilion. The door was unlocked and yielded easily. She walked in, and Cesar followed.

'This is our chance to talk,' she said.

Cesar closed the door behind them. Leaning back against it, he stared at her. 'Is this what you want?'

It took a single step in either direction to answer his question. She stepped forward.

Cesar dipped his head and brushed her lips with his. 'You'd better not take advantage of me,' she whispered.

'I'd say the shoe was on the other foot.'

But he made the next move, moving in for a gentle, lingering kiss, and as he teased the seam of her lips apart, an overwhelming surge of hunger consumed her.

The moment was right. Reaching up, she linked her hands behind his neck.

Looping her hair around her fist, Cesar drew her head back. 'I've always loved chocolate.'

'It must have melted in my hand,' she admitted between whimpers of pleasure.

'I don't care how it got there,' he assured her, lavishing kisses on her neck, her chin, her cheeks, and finally her lips. 'Only that I get to lick it off.'

Her answer was to press her body against his. Leaning into him, she parted her lips, inviting the invasion of his tongue.

Cesar unleashed a tiger inside her. The fact that she was inexperienced, and definitely playing with fire, meant nothing to her now.

All she could think of was keeping him close so he deepened the kiss. Their bodies acted independently, seeking each other greedily and fiercely, while throaty sounds of pleasure flew from her lips.

'I think you want this,' Cesar observed as he teased her with more and more kisses.

'You think?' she whispered as she began to undress him.

There was a moment's pause when they stared at each other as if for the first time, and then clothes were flying everywhere.

Cesar was even more beautiful than she had imagined, though in a harsh and rugged way. With a lazy smile, he mapped her breasts, delivering exquisite pleasure that left her incapable of speech. Sounds of encouragement flew from her throat when he tormented her nipples into tight buds of sensation.

'You have magnificent breasts,' Cesar commented matter-of-factly.

'I'm glad you approve.'

He laughed in a way that made sensation travel from her breasts to the sweet spot between her legs. 'Your nipples are so responsive—like the rest of you, I'm guessing?'

'You wouldn't be wrong,' she admitted.

Cesar's voice was a seduction in itself, and made her hungry for more. Naked skin to naked skin was all she could think about. Instinct said Cesar would pleasure her as no one else could.

Swinging her into his arms, he carried her across to a well-padded banquette. But seduction was not on his mind. 'You wanted to talk to me?' he prompted.

Cesar's swift change of pace was a reminder to keep her wits about her, or this opportunity to talk would be wasted. Having proved he could seduce her with little or no effort at all, Cesar had put that one aside in favour of interrogation.

'I don't have all night,' he said, confirming this.

'I apologise for the article, but there was a very good reason for it.'

'What reason could there possibly be?' His voice was cool, his expression unyielding. 'Did you expect me to seduce you and then forget what you'd done? Is that why you agreed to come with me into the garden?'

'That was never my intention.' Her voice

was heated, and she had wanted a civilised talk. Why could they never meet without passion of getting in the way? 'I was just grateful to have an opportunity to talk to you. Please believe me when I tell you that everything is not as it seems.'

'So you didn't write the article, as you didn't kiss me just now?'

'If you only knew the truth,' she protested.

'How I'd love to know the truth, but as you show no sign of sharing your version of it any time soon—'

'My version of it?' she exclaimed. 'And now you're leaving?'

'Why should I stay?' Cesar demanded from the door.

'Please, I—'

'You what?' he said coldly.

'Please listen to me,' she begged softly. 'I needed that money for my retreat.'

'Which I already knew. I thought you had something new to say.'

'I was invited to submit an article to a well-known newspaper.'

'A scandal sheet,' Cesar derided. 'And that's not news to me.'

'Read by millions,' she countered firmly.

He dismissed this with an indifferent gesture.

'That means it paid well,' she explained. 'I don't expect you to understand what it feels like to be short of money.'

'Oh, really?' Cesar demanded cuttingly. 'That only shows how little you know me.'

And how would she ever learn, when Cesar was notoriously reserved about his past? 'I can't pretend to have suffered as a child,' she admitted, 'Which was why it was so hard for Xander when our parents were killed. We had an idyllic childhood, and you think that's going to go on for ever. I never imagined it could end so abruptly.'

'Yet you suffered this loss, and went on to discard the principles your parents must have instilled in you. How could you do that, Sofia, just to raise money? I find it hard to believe that, with the Acosta name behind you, banks didn't flock to help. Or was it glory you were seeking? To see your name in print at any cost?'

'The banks had already helped as much as they were prepared to. I'd reached my limit,' she explained. 'I thought it would be easy to write an article with mass appeal—no details, no scandal, just a taste of the glamour that follows you and my brothers around. I didn't see any harm in it—'

'Until it was too late?' Cesar interrupted. 'By which time you had banked the money.' He held up his hand when she started to explain. 'For the sake of the charities we must move past that. Including you in the team will swell the crowds. They'll come to see how things have worked out between us, so we'll put on an act as we have done tonight. It shouldn't be so difficult. We've had our dress rehearsal, but don't ever mistake good manners for forgiveness. Do I make myself clear?'

'Perfectly.'

'Then I'll bid you goodnight.'

The ringing silence inside the pavilion seemed to last long after Cesar had gone. They were no closer to understanding each other than they had been at the start of the evening, but she had exposed how she felt about Cesar, only for him to turn and walk away.

CHAPTER SIX

TEAM LOBOS AND their associated staff left Rome for Cesar's breeding and training ranch in the far north west of Italy the day after the banquet. There were no unnecessary frills in this residence, though everything was of the highest quality. The facility was entirely dedicated to the well-being of the horses. As well as countless other animals, Cesar allowed as a pack of his favourite dogs circled his legs, looking for fuss and for treats. He didn't disappoint them. Kneeling down so he was at their level, he lavished affection on his most loyal friends.

'You still have some admirers, I see...'

His hackles rose at the sound of Sofia's voice. She was like a cork that never stayed down for long.

'Ready for battle?'

This was the far more welcome voice of Sofia's brother Dante. 'Dante!'

He sprang up and they embraced fiercely. The other Spanish Acosta brothers took their turns. Fearless, and loyal to a fault, it was a shame their sister failed to share the same brand of loyalty.

He stood back. 'You all know my sister Olivia...' Olivia raised a laugh as she gave a mock bow. 'And Jess, Dante's wife.' At his prompt, an attractive redhead joined Cesar and Dante in the centre of the arena. 'Jess is also a top-flight physiotherapist and trainer, and I know we're all going to enjoy her punishing exercises.'

Jess acknowledged the chorus of catcalls with a lopsided grin. 'Thank you for the glowing recommendation, but we have to win the tournament before I believe your praise. Until then, all I can promise is hard, relentless training.' She waited for the comic groans to die down before revealing, I'll be working in tandem with another person here... Sofia...?'

As Sofia stepped forward, Cesar ground his teeth. What the hell?

'What is the meaning of this?' he demanded.

'The meaning?' Jess enquired, laughing, no doubt thinking he was joking. 'I don't know anyone better than Sofia for building team spirit. I've seen her work with her brothers, don't forget. And Sofia's organisational skills are second to none.' Jess looked at him with surprise when he failed to stifle a scoffing huff. 'That's why her retreat is such a success,' Jess continued doggedly, with a piercing look at him. 'Anyone who has experienced Sofia's retreat can tell you the benefits. They learn to live life to the full again, and they learn to trust.'

'Excellent,' he bit out. He'd heard enough of the nonsense. Only the calming presence of Dante at his side, and the grimly set faces of those of Sofia's brothers who didn't care to hear her praised went some way to soothing his frayed temper. 'We're relying on you, Jess,' he emphasised, 'for our training regime in the run-up to the matches.'

In his peripheral vision he saw Sofia stiffen but Jess continued, undaunted. 'Without complete trust between team members you can ride the best ponies in the world and field the fittest, sharpest players, but if there isn't proper communication between each member of the team—the kind of communication that doesn't need anyone to shout for the ball, or make it clear that their horse is tiring, because your fellow players know exactly where you are, how you stand, and who best to shoot the ball to—your play will never be as dynamic or as fluid as it needs to be.'

Jess talked good sense, but he still failed to see what part Sofia had to play in this. 'I invited you to become a member of this team for the duration of the charity matches,' he murmured in Sofia's ear, 'but I don't recall hiring you to help with training.'

'You didn't have to hire me,' she informed him pleasantly. 'I'm here because Jess asked me to help her, which I'm more than willing to do.'

The irony was that as Sofia didn't work for him, he couldn't fire her, even if he wanted to. No wonder he preferred binding contracts where anyone who failed to meet the mark could be let go without a fuss.

Sofia began to address the group as cool as you like. 'We're lucky to have this chance to practise together. I know how busy you all are. Knowing your team members inside out, so you're aware of their strengths and weaknesses, as well as how they play the game, will give us the advantage we need.'

He was rocked back on his heels by the sight of two women taking centre stage, as if he were a newcomer to the game. 'That's enough talking,' he decreed with a closing gesture. 'This is nothing we don't know. We're professionals. We adapt. And now we work.'

Jess worked them hard. Truthfully, Sofia was finding it hard to keep up with Cesar and her brothers, but there was no way she going to let the side down. Olivia and Jess were as determined as she was to prove their worth to the team. Jess managed to make training fun. Galloping at full stretch, leaning over the side of her pony to snatch up a can that appeared to have invisible legs was something Sofia hadn't done since she was a child. No one fell off, though noisy hilarity and catcalls released a lot of the initial tension. By the time that morning's session was over, Sofia could do little more than slide down the side of her pony in exhaustion. But neither could she remember enjoying herself so much in a long time.

'Can I help you with that?'

She turned to see Cesar lounging back against the wall, watching her. Removing tack from a spirited pony was normally a straightforward operation, but today the bridle seemed to weigh a ton and her mount was overly keen to be turned out into the field.

'You look as if your knees are about to buckle,' Cesar remarked as she almost lost her footing.

'I can manage, thank you.'

'But you don't have to,' he pointed out, and taking the saddle out of her arms he led the way to the tack room where the others in the team were waiting. 'I've arranged entertainment for later,' he announced when everything was safely stowed away.

'So long as it doesn't involve moving,' Olivia groaned. 'I don't need *entertainment*. I need a long, hot bath.'

'You can have both,' Cesar promised.

Olivia grunted disbelievingly but Jess exclaimed, 'Wonderful!' as she linked arms with her husband.

Infected by Jess's enthusiasm, Sofia smiled too. 'If I don't fall asleep in the bath, I'll be there,' she promised.

'I'll save you a place,' Cesar offered, surprising everyone, not least himself, Sofia suspected when she caught the brief flash of surprise on his face.

If she'd hoped for something more—a glimmer of warmth in his eyes, for instance—she was disappointed. There was nothing in Cesar's expression when he looked her way but the same coolness and suspicion.

He sluiced down in the yard. Everyone else had retired to their rooms to rest, clean up and prepare for the evening ahead. His grooms had taken charge of the ponies, but he chose to check everything twice. The ponies had worked as hard if not harder than their riders, and also deserved a reward.

Raking his hair back, he slung his top over his still-damp shoulders and entered the state-of-the-art building where his beloved animals were kept. He prided himself on the fact that this accommodation was as good as that of his guests.

'Sofia?' He might have known.

'Cesar!' She seemed equally shocked. 'I was just checking the ponies were settled for the night,' she explained.

'I'd have put a top on if I'd known you were here.'

She angled her chin to stare at him boldly. 'Would you?'

Silence fell as they stared at each other. In fairness, Sofia had worked as hard as anyone and yet here she was, tending to the horses when she could have been indulging in a long, hot bath.

Must she moisten her lips like that?

He held her stare. 'Don't you want to rest before the evening entertainment? "Freshen up"?' he suggested.

She grinned. 'Was that a hint?'

He ignored the comment. 'In honour of your family I've brought over a group of flamenco dancers from Andalucía.'

'That was very nice of you. Just don't let my brothers sing,' she warned with a slanting smile.

It was almost nothing, perhaps a brief window into another side of Sofia: a fun side, a family side, a carefree side of a woman he hadn't seen so far.

'Best leave singing to the professionals,' she said.

'How about you?' he asked. 'It's your tradition. Will you dance?'

'Flamenco?' she exclaimed. 'You just try and stop me.'

He had no intention of doing so, he mused as Sofia struck a pose. She looked so beautiful—alluring beyond belief. The sight of her wreaked havoc on his groin. 'Tonight promises to be one to remember.'

'For all the right reasons, I hope?' she countered.

He stared into her eyes. She pleased and infuriated him in equal measure. How could she appear so frank and open after everything she'd done? If he judged Sofia by right here, right now, he'd say she was a free spirit who loved nothing more than to ride hard and live to help others. What had happened to change that? Surely she couldn't have turned into a self-serving schemer overnight?

She shrugged when he didn't answer and ended on a flippant note. 'I'll try hard not to disappoint you,' she promised with one last flashing glance.

He watched as she walked away. What was she playing at now? Sofia Acosta was as sharp as a bag of monkeys, and twice as resourceful. She was determined to keep her retreat afloat, and had already shown she would stop at nothing to do that.

Yet still he wanted her.

Why not? he mused as he watched as Sofia met his sister Olivia halfway across the yard and fell into conversation with her. Both women were beautiful, and as spirited as his most challenging mare. With a back view as impressive as her front, he loved the way Sofia strode out. He loved the sway in her shapely body. Not for the first time, he thought her perfect. Would he sleep with the enemy? Why not? But first he must unravel the enigma that was Sofia Acosta. In spite of everything that had gone before, he wanted to know her both in and out of bed.

Nope. She hadn't packed a party dress suitable for a flamenco party. All she had in her zip-up case were numerous pairs of jodhpurs and jeans in varying stages of disrepair, a stack of clean tops, two spare pairs of PJs, toiletries and comfortable underwear that could in no way be described as glamorous. This was a training camp after all. Not that it was a typical training camp. Everything was high quality and practical, but the suite of rooms Sofia had been directed to, for instance, contained enough tech to satisfy even her brothers. There was also every muscle-easing balm and potion known to man in the bathroom, which she intended to take full and luxurious advantage of. A separate room was devoted to massage, and there was a sauna, as well as a steam room and an ice bath. The latter she was determined to swerve.

She chose bubbles.

The bath was huge. The warm water was plentiful, and the selection of fragrances mind-blowing. She could happily have remained soaking all night, without the prospect of a party. Would Cesar be relaxed in an informal setting or would he still be cool and unreadable? Numerous images flashed through her mind, but for this one night she was going to forget the damning article and have fun.

Which meant sorting out an outfit for the party.

No problem, Sofia reflected as she towelled down. She had a tongue in her head and an exuberant group of *gitanos* had arrived from the mountains of Andalucía to entertain them. She could hear them in the courtyard now. There was a possibility they might have heard of her mother. Keeping the tradition of flamenco alive required a tight-knit if widespread community.

It had been on a night similar to this that Sofia's aristocratic Acosta father had met his future wife. Sofia's mother had danced for him and, according to her father, the firelight had not been able to compete with the fire in her mother's eyes. It remained to be seen if tonight would be a damp squib for Sofia, or whether the traditional music and dance would thrill everyone with its upbeat message.

Sofia was welcomed into the *gitanos'* fold like a long-lost sister, daughter, friend. She was deeply touched by how many women clustered around to help her pick out a gown. Cesar had housed the performers in some of the most luxurious accommodation so there was plenty of room for all the women and Sofia to gather, and plenty of room to prepare properly, which was fortunate as Sofia's hair alone took a good deal of taming and grooming before it could be confined in the severe style worn by all the women. The last touch was an ornate comb for her hair, decorated with sparkling paste jewels, which held a flowing black lace mantilla in place. There was only one problem, in that Sofia's new friends seemed to think that she would be one of the star performers tonight. 'Your mother's talent was legendary,' the head dancer told her. 'You can't refuse.'

Neither would she. 'Of course I'll dance,' she agreed with a flutter of nerves.

She tried out a few steps, and it was a relief to find that the childhood lessons from her mother had not deserted her.

'And you must use a fan,' one of the older women insisted. 'The language of the fan is universal.'

And dangerous, Sofia reflected as she stared at the glorious bright red fan the woman wanted her to use. Flamenco was a sensual dance that ebbed and flowed as smoothly as silk, with rhythmic stamps to punctuate the dancer's movements. This built tension and excitement, while a fan allowed grace and style to soften the repeated clatter of heels on wood. But a fan must always be used with discretion, Sofia remembered her mother telling her, as it increased the charm of the dancer's spell.

She was taken aback when she caught sight of herself in a mirror, and thanked the women who'd helped her profusely. 'I can't believe the transformation!' she exclaimed, as she took in the sight of her hourglass figure in a tight-fitting black and white dress. With its frills and ruffles—which she never, ever wore normally—the costume made her feel like a different person, one who was bold and who never suffered from doubt.

What would her brothers make of seeing her on stage? Whatever their differences, she was confident they'd cheer her on. She was an Acosta. They were family, and it was this deep and abiding love that would always protect her. Her brothers might think she had abused that love, and she could only hope that one day they would forgive her.

And Cesar? What would he think when he saw her on stage?

When he entered the room her stomach clenched with nerves at the thought of performing in front of him.

CHAPTER SEVEN

'I'VE COME TO make sure you all have everything you need,' he said, taking in Sofia's much-changed appearance with interest. 'If there's anything more I can do for you,' he added, 'please let me know.'

The soft whir of the spurs on her fan as she opened it drew his attention. 'I didn't expect to find you here. Are you performing tonight? I have to say the costume suits you.'

'This is all thanks to my new friends,' she explained as the women who had helped her watched on. 'My mother's people,' she explained, remembering how her mother had told her to take compliments gracefully and always be proud of who she was. Composing her features into something less wistful, she raised her chin and said, 'Thank you.'

'So I will see you dance tonight,' Cesar concluded.

'You will,' she confirmed, thinking him

so rampantly male it would be hard to concentrate on anything while he was watching. But behind that compelling persona she saw genuine interest fire in his eyes. This was a chance to make her mother proud, and her brothers too. She couldn't influence Cesar. His thoughts were up to him.

She was surprised when he waited behind to escort her. 'Will you allow me?' he asked.

'Do I have a choice?' she teased.

He linked her arm through his. 'None,' he confirmed.

The party was being held outside, where a huge bonfire lit up the night. The stage was set at a safe distance in front of it, backlighting the performers with soaring flames. A backdrop of mountains and a soundscape of owls could lead some to think this a romantic setting. Not Sofia, who had so much to prove, though it was certainly rare to have a flamenco performance in this part of Italy, with Apennine wolves howling in the background, as if they agreed that she'd better not mess this up.

'Did you organise the wolf chorus especially for Team Lobos?' Dante enquired with amusement as he and Jess came over to greet Cesar and Sofia.

'My friends never disappoint me,' Cesar confirmed dryly. 'They are no doubt as curious and as excited as we are, especially as we're so close to their mountain home.'

It was an elemental setting, Sofia realised as she looked around, and as such was the perfect setting for Cesar.

'Are you dancing tonight?' Dante asked, taking in her costume.

'That's the price I have to pay for borrowing one of these fabulous dresses,' she admitted, 'though I hope I can remember the steps our mother taught me.'

'You will,' Dante said confidently.

She had to now.

'No one persuades Sofia to do anything she doesn't want to do,' Cesar commented, which earned him a look and a shrug from Dante. 'Enjoy the party,' he added.

Just how much she would enjoy the party remained to be seen.

* * *

There must have been something in the air that night, or maybe it was the fabulous red fan, casting its promised spell. Surrounded by her mother's people, Sofia felt able to express herself fully and freely, perhaps for the first time since she'd lost her mother. Tears rolled unchecked down her cheeks at one point while she danced, for all the things they could no longer share, and when the final chord sounded and the main dancer came on stage, she took Sofia in her arms to whisper, 'Your mother would be very proud of you. And remember that as we cry when we lose someone, we live on in their honour to laugh and make love, and live fully again.'

And then the crowd went wild, and called for an encore.

There comes a point at the end of an impassioned flamenco solo when the dancer, having expended every last drop of emotion, cries out, *'Duende!'* and drops to the floor. He was waiting at the side ready to give his congratulatory speech once Sofia had finished dancing when that moment occurred. Sofia struck her final pose, and then allowed her limbs to soften and her face to relax as she sank to the ground.

'*Duende!*'

The audience rewarded Sofia with rapturous applause. Duende perfectly expressed the heightened emotions he'd witnessed on stage, and he was cheering with the rest. There couldn't be a single person present she hadn't touched in some way.

Sofia was an extraordinary performer. The story she'd told through the medium of dance was one that everyone could relate to at some point. The mask she showed to the world had dropped away, leaving Sofia totally exposed and vulnerable. He might have had every reason to mistrust her in the past, but what he'd seen made him want to re-evaluate what he knew of.

'Congratulations!' he exclaimed as he raised her to her feet.

'I have my mother to thank.' Her eyes were shining with happy memories as she looked back into the past. 'My mother believed in the power of dance, saying music is a power for good.'

'Your mother was right, and you certainly

convinced everyone here,' he admitted as he led her forward to take another bow. 'You surprised me tonight,' he confessed once they were out of the spotlight.

'Well, we don't know that much about each other, do we, Cesar?' she said as she lifted her chin to search his eyes. 'All we know is what we see now, and what rumour suggests is fact. Who knows how many more surprises are in store?'

'Just don't write another article,' he cautioned with a lift of his brow.

Her face fell, making him wish he hadn't said it. Couldn't he even allow her to enjoy this moment of triumph?

'I promise I won't,' she said in all seriousness.

'Forget it,' he rapped, angry with himself for being so crass. 'Take your applause. You've earned it.'

He left Sofia with her newly won admirers, most of whom were young dancers dressed in traditional costume, all wanting autographs and selfies with Sofia.

'I'll be with your brothers if you need me.' He jerked his chin towards the crowded bar area, feeling vaguely discomfited as he accepted he could have handled this better.

'I felt like a fraud,' Sofia told him some time later when she had returned to his side.'

'I don't know why,' he said as he drew her away from the boisterous crowd to find a quieter spot.

'I haven't done anything like this in years,' she admitted. 'Not since I was a little girl, in fact.'

'Then perhaps you should do more,' he suggested.

'I'll bring you up on stage next time,' she threatened.

'You may regret that.'

'I'm prepared to chance it,' she shot back.

'Well, now...'

'Now?' she pressed.

'I must get back to the rest of my guests. If you will excuse me?'

'Of course,' she said faintly. And was that regret?

Sofia barely had chance to speak to Cesar for the next part of the night. It was a great party, so many people to talk to. Her brothers were swept up in a good-natured crowd, relaxing and enjoying themselves, and it felt so good to Sofia to relax and unwind. Escape the web of intrigue into which she'd inadvertently become embroiled when she'd written that article. Doing nothing more complicated than talking and laughing and dancing, she couldn't have enjoyed herself more—or so she thought until Cesar stepped forward to make a short speech.

'We've had a wonderful night of entertainment, for which I'm immensely grateful,' he declared. 'And now it's time for everyone to enjoy themselves, performers and guests alike. So I invite you to party, but not too hard because tomorrow the real work on match fitness begins.'

The usual chorus of groans greeted this statement, though it didn't seem to stop anyone enjoying the party.

'But before we start training again,' Cesar added, 'I'm claiming my right to dance with the star performer.'

Me? The thought of Cesar's body enfolding hers, and without the need for pretence this time, made Sofia's heart riot. She had to remind herself that this was just an innocent dance, and when it finished she'd return to her quarters, take a shower and go to bed.

Who was she kidding?

Difficult questions could wait until later.

Her body melted from the inside out when Cesar took her into his arms. Heat fizzed through her veins, bringing everything into sharp focus. Her awareness level soared. They fitted so well together, which didn't make sense when Cesar was twice her size. But it was a fact, she realised as he led and she followed. 'Don't get used to shepherding me around the floor,' she warned with amusement born of nerves.

'I don't notice too much resistance,' he remarked. 'You're an excellent dancer, and I enjoy using my body.'

Her senses were in freefall now Cesar's rampantly male body was aligned with hers. The urge to move and rub herself against him was constant—one she knew she had to resist.

'Relax,' he murmured, drawing her closer still. 'Or stop dancing. It's your choice. We're not acting now so there's no need to pretend, if you don't want to.'

He was giving her an out she didn't want. Up to now her hand had remained unmoving in his, while her body was as unresponsive as she could make it, but the thought of leaving Cesar and walking away forced her fingers to ease in his as she consciously relaxed her shoulders. Cesar responded by linking their fingers, which she found both intimate and exciting. His other hand was lodged in the small of her back, his fingers resting on the topmost swell of her buttocks.

Waves of want flooded her. They were so close they shared the same breath, the same air, but was this sensible or would it leave her with more unanswered questions? 'We've got training tomorrow,' she reminded them both. 'I should be thinking about bed.' The insistent rhythmic strum of guitars called her a liar. She wanted nothing more than to stay and dance with Cesar.

Releasing her as the music reached a crescendo and finally stopped, Cesar stepped back. 'I'll see you back to the house.'

'You can't leave your guests,' she pointed out.

'I doubt anyone will even notice that I've gone,' Cesar insisted as he steered her away.

So speaks the man who has no idea of the effect he has on people, Sofia reflected as she noticed how many of their fellow dancers glanced at Cesar as they left the improvised dance floor. His type of machismo could electrify a room. 'I don't need you to take me back,' she insisted, avoiding his gaze. She glanced at the last place she'd seen her brothers. They would normally take her back, but they weren't even looking her way.

'Just tell me what you want,' Cesar prompted.

His grip on her wrist might be gentle but the look in Cesar's eyes was not at all safe. What did she want? What was he offering? To be alone with him? The connection between them fired as they stared at each other.

Just for one night. That's all it would be.

They didn't make it as far as the ranch house or even the guest quarters. The hay barn loomed. The building was in darkness when they arrived. Before she could lift the latch, Cesar had swung her round, and with his arms bracketing either side of her face he kissed her hungrily and she kissed him back.

'No,' he rapped as her body enthusiastically took the lead. 'Not here. Not with you dressed like this. '

He was right. The mantilla she was wearing was held in place by a large, ornate hair comb, and the flamenco dress fitted her like a second skin.

Sweeping her into his arms, Cesar shouldered the door and carried her inside the shaded interior where the air was warm and fragrant, and countless dust motes danced on moonbeams. There was nothing to compare with the scent of stacked hay, unless it was the scent of Cesar, Sofia concluded as he set her down gently on a sweet-smelling bed of clean hay.

'You should never tie your hair back,' he said as he removed the comb and mantilla with dextrous skill. 'There should be a law against it.'

She couldn't believe how carefully he rearranged her severely drawn-back hair, finger-combing it until it hung in its usual tumbling disorder. Was this a man she could confide in, or was she fooling herself again? History showed her to be woefully lacking when it came to good judgement.

She needn't have worried. With the removal of her clothes tension between them gradually relaxed and in its place came playful intimacy. Nothing that had happened in the past seemed relevant. Only this moment mattered. Until he hit a sweet spot on her neck.

'You're like a highly strung pony, always ready to bolt,' Cesar observed huskily.

'Where would I bolt to?'

'Back to the party?' he suggested.

'In my underwear?'

'What remains of it,' he commented with amusement. 'What am I going to do with you, Sofia Acosta?'

'Didn't you bring your clipboard?'

Cesar stared at her for a moment then laughed. 'Tell me what you want,' he insisted.

Her heart was thumping. The menu was tempting. Cesar was dressed in low-slung, snug-fitting jeans that displayed more than a few tantalising inches of hard, toned flesh.

No wonder her body was responding by aching and yearning.

She didn't move when he settled himself over her, braced on muscular arms.

Where to start?

'Kiss me?' she suggested.

CHAPTER EIGHT

SHE COULD NEVER have predicted what a simple request to kiss her would entail. Starting with her feet, Cesar kissed the soles, her ankles, her calves and finally her thighs, until she thought she would go mad with waiting. Locking stares, he moved past her thighs. If the attention he'd given the rest of her legs was anything to go by...

A soft cry escaped her lips when he murmured, 'Look at me.'

Staring into his eyes was the most erotic experience of her life. It was as if Cesar could see through her to every thought and feeling she had. When he found her and cupped her, she almost lost control, but his touch was so light, too light, and she wanted more. Covering his hand with hers, she demanded more. It wasn't a question of boldness now but more a lifesaver like the air she breathed. It only took a moment and she was lost.

'Greedy,' Cesar murmured as she bucked uncontrollably in the throes of a most powerful release. Unable to control her cries of pleasure, she could only respond by instinct, grateful that he used one hand to palm her buttocks and hold her in place, while he extended her pleasure with his other hand.

'More?' he queried with low, husky, sexy amusement when she was quiet again. Her answer was to reach for the waistband of his jeans. Dealing with the belt first, she ripped it out of its loops and tossed it aside. Next came the zipper, but Cesar took over and dealt with that with efficient speed.

'I need you to do something for me now,' he said.

'Anything,' she offered fiercely.

'Your task is to do nothing at all. Your only goal is to float and feel.'

As he spoke, Cesar removed her bra, only pausing to lavish attention on her breasts before removing her tiny thong. Stripping off his jeans, he moved over her.

Moving between her legs, he teased her with the tip of his erection. But just when she was sure she was ready, he drew back.

Resting her legs wide on his shoulders, he pressed her back onto the hay. 'Remember what I told you?'

A ragged sigh escaped her as Cesar dipped his head. After that first release it was a surprise to discover how easily he could make her needy again. She fell quickly, screaming into ecstasy, and the drowning waves of pleasure went on and on. 'How do you do that?' she asked when she had the breath to do so.

Laughing softly, Cesar cupped her buttocks to raise her to his mouth.

He took her gently because Sofia was inexperienced. It rested on him to set the pace. Left to herself she would scramble all over him, and it would be done in moments. He wanted more for her than that. Delay was the servant of pleasure, and Sofia was like a flower unfurling, a process that should never be rushed.

Giving her more, and then a little more still, while she clung to him, her eyes telling him everything he needed to know. She was apprehensive but eager. She wanted him, wanted this, but wasn't quite sure if she could handle it, handle him. He was so big and she was so small. He could practically see these thoughts flashing through her mind. To help ease her concerns, he spoke soft words of encouragement in his own tongue, until gradually she relaxed enough for her hands to stop gripping him like vices. They would soon close on him again when she urged him on to give her the greatest pleasure of all.

When she rested her arms above her head in an attitude of complete trust, he knew she was ready. Protecting them both, he enclosed her wrists in one big fist and cupped her buttocks with his other hand to guide her onto him. Nudging her thighs apart, he sank a little deeper, and then a little deeper still.

'Relax... *Rilassati, tesoro... Non aver paura. Non ti farei mai del male...* Don't be frightened. I would never hurt you.'

'I'm not frightened,' she assured him, though her breathing was hectic and her voice was unsteady, which told him the exactly opposite.

Easing Sofia's fear was paramount. Releasing her wrists, he made sure she made the transition from tension and concern to hunger and need within the space of a few well-judged strokes.

'Ah, yes, yes!' she exclaimed, and, exactly as he had anticipated, she reached for his buttocks to urge him on.

He rested deep, and waited to allow Sofia to become used to the new sensation. Then he gently massaged her by rotating his hips. That was her flash point. She lost control immediately, falling with excited screams of pleasure as she experienced the new and hugely increased sensation of release while he filled her. Her inner muscles attempted to suck him dry, but he had control to spare when it came to Sofia.

'*Non ancora, il mio piccolo micio*—not yet, my little wildcat,' he insisted, holding her still as she battled to bring him release.

'When? You have to! It's amazing,' she insisted on a great exhalation of breath. 'I mean, I realise that you know that, but—'

'But?' he queried with amusement as he began to move again.

'Don't expect me to speak now,' she protested on a ragged breath.

'I don't. I expect you only to—'

'Float and feel,' she remembered, heaving another great sigh of pleasure as he moved faster, the finish of each stroke a little firmer each time.

When she fell again he laughed softly against her hair. She took an age to come down. 'You are the greediest person I've ever known.'

'I don't want to know about *others*,' she assured him with all the old fire.

'What others?' he demanded, lifting his head to stare her in the eyes. 'There is only one Sofia.'

Wasn't that the truth? Sofia accepted as reality raised its ugly head—or in this case multiple beautiful heads, all perfectly coiffed and exquisitely made up, as befitted the women in the life of one of the world's most eligible bachelors.

So why was Cesar with her? Was this revenge? Was he proving a point? She hoped not, because for her this was so much more. It was an exercise in trust.

Searching Cesar's eyes, she found what looked like genuine concern, but she didn't want his pity. She'd had enough of being petted by her brothers as if she were their favourite puppy, only to be kicked out without a chance to explain her misguided actions. She longed for a man who treated her as his equal, and who would expect her to account for what she'd done. A man who would listen and maybe understand. She wanted to believe that man was Cesar, and was forced to remind herself that sex was second nature to Cesar, like eating or breathing.

'You will sleep with me tonight,' he decreed.

She stared up with surprise. 'I'll sleep in my own bed,' she stated. 'We both have to work first thing.'

A smile tugged at one corner of his mouth. 'Are you saying that if you stay with me no work will be done?'

'Not the right type of work,' she said as she reached for her clothes.

Capturing her hands in his, Cesar nuzzled her neck, her mouth, her cheeks with his sharp stubble, until she couldn't bring herself to leave. She wanted to stay with him, so they could grow closer in every way there was.

There was a rustle of foil, and then he

turned her so her back was to his chest. 'I promise you'll sleep tonight,' he murmured, the sexy smile in his voice, encouraging her, as before, to lose control.

Had she really chosen her bed over his? Had that encounter in the hay barn really happened?

Determined to cling to reason, she reasoned that Cesar had made no attempt to prevent her leaving. He took his pleasure where he found it—no strings, no consequences, and she was a fool if she read anything more into it than that. But reason wasn't enough to stop her hurting and wanting, or longing for a different type of closeness with Cesar. Leaning back against her bedroom door, eyes tightly shut and with her body still singing with remembered pleasure, she could only rail silently against yet another missed opportunity for them to talk.

Had Cesar been looking for conversation?

She hadn't exactly been talkative herself. If things had been different, if the regime they'd embarked on in preparation for the matches hadn't been so demanding...

If only, if only, if only. But would you have stated your case and taken the consequences, whatever they might be?

If there was a major fallout between them, it would impact the whole team, and with the charity matches coming up fast none of them needed more ripples right now.

So you're burying it? What about the plan to thwart your blackmailer?

Grinding her teeth, as if that would shut out her inner critic, she determined to keep a tight rein on her emotions, and only tell Cesar the whole story when launching preventative measures against the blackmailer would have minimum impact on anyone else.

What about all those people you're supposed to be protecting? The people at your retreat, your brothers, Cesar?

A soft yelp of desperation escaped her throat. Her retreat was full to capacity with vulnerable people. She'd been looking for ways to open another—

And now?

Pulling away from the door, she headed out. She found Cesar in the deserted kitchen, drinking coffee and demolishing a pizza. 'I'm sorry to disturb you.'

'You're not.'

The flatness of his statement pinned her to the spot. There was no warmth in his eyes and no recollection of remembered pleasure, as far as she could tell. Cesar had sated one of his needs and now he was sating another... with pizza.

So retreat or advance. Your choice.

She moved deeper into the room. 'I'm not here for the reason you suppose.'

'And what is that?'

Holding his black stare was a challenge she met gladly, though there was no hint of the generous lover Cesar had been only a short time before.

'What am I thinking?' he pressed.

'That I've changed my mind about spending the night with you?'

A few long seconds passed, during which Cesar drank more coffee and ate more pizza. 'Why would you do that?' he asked, his sharp gaze suspicious. 'The little I know about you says you only do what you want to do, when you want to do it.'

The sudden realisation that Cesar thought her as coldblooded as him came as an unpleasant shock, but what else could he think after reading the article she had supposedly written?

The one thing she must not do was risk turning this into a confrontation. She needed help, and couldn't be too proud to ask him. 'I need to talk to you—really talk to you,' she explained. 'Now would be good, if that's okay with you? It's important, Cesar,' she stressed when he shrugged.

'Have you finally decided to apologise for the article?' he suggested with a keen, sideways look.

'I can explain how it came about, and was then changed without my knowledge before it went to print.'

'That's some story. You want me to believe you're an innocent dupe,' he suggested. 'Forgive me if I find that hard to believe.'

'Cesar, please—'

'You must excuse me.' He pushed away from the counter. 'I'm heading off to bed. I suggest you do the same. As you mentioned before, we have training tomorrow.'

She stared at the door long after Cesar had closed it behind him. Explaining her actions wouldn't be easy. Cesar wasn't easy. But what in life was? She would just have to find another way.

He couldn't forgive her, and had only firmed his resolve. Everything about Sofia fired him up—to anger, to passion, to disgust. She might be the first member of the team to arrive each morning for training, and the last to dismount when each day's demanding session was over, but she hadn't needed to write that article, and had clearly given no thought to the harm it would do.

It was still possible to enjoy her. They enjoyed each other. That was something separate. It was a simple arrangement between them, with no demands beyond those of mutual pleasure on either side.

The next day's training went well, though he'd had a sleepless night. Judging by the dark circles around her eyes, Sofia hadn't slept well either. Each time their stares clashed, electricity fired between them. It was only a matter of time before he had her again. Primal hunger needed an outlet. She knew that as well as he. As dutiful about training as Sofia undoubtedly was, she was also a hot-blooded woman and the thought of sinking deep into her exquisite warmth provided him with the most delicious torture throughout a satisfyingly testing day.

He was alone in the stables when she found him after training. The topic she chose to open with was not what he had expected. 'You want to talk about the article?' he queried, pulling his head back with surprise.

'And this time have you listen,' she insisted.

He raised a brow.

'Sorry. That sounded harsh.'

Sofia taking an unusual tack shouldn't surprise him, but the fact that her heated glances had either meant nothing or he'd imagined them, which was unlikely, irritated him. Continuing to check his pony's legs, he waited to hear what she had to say.

She joined him in the stall, where there was no sound apart from his mount contentedly munching. Their teammates were already refuelling in the ranch house, so they were alone.

'I want to explain. I have to,' she insisted. 'I can't stand this tension between us. And what's the point of waiting for the right time when the right time never comes?' She caught hold of his elbow when he stood up to go. 'Cesar—'

He pinned her with a cold glance. 'Well? What do you want to say to me?'

As they stared at each other something changed in her eyes. Her body softened, and the words she had been about to say froze on her lips. 'No,' she whispered huskily, keeping eye contact.

'Yes,' he argued softly. He'd never had a problem in recognising or responding to the needs of his body.

'We must talk,' she insisted in a breathy whisper.

Her eyes were black, her lips were swollen, and her breathing was growing increasingly rapid. 'All you need to say is yes,' he insisted in the same low tone.

She was instantly in the moment when he found her with his hand. Her heat reached him through her breeches. 'This is what you need,' he explained as his fingers went to work. But she hadn't finished with surprises yet.

'This is what we both need,' she insisted, eyes blazing a challenge into his.

When she was done, she sank against him, spent. She'd used him. That was okay with him. Kissing her, he undressed her. She saw to the button at the top of his jeans. Wrapping her hands around him, she smiled and voiced her pleasure, as if he had provided her with all the delights of the world in one jutting member.

Having protected them both, he thrust forward. They exclaimed with relief. After a moment or two of basking in sensation, he lifted her, so she could lock her legs around his waist while he pounded into her. From there it was a crazy, furious ride towards the goal they were both seeking, and when they reached it, it was stunning in its ferocity for both of them.

'Again?' he suggested as Sofia groaned and writhed in his arms, biting her fingers into his muscles.

Her answer was to work her hips greedily against his, but to his surprise this felt like

more than sex, more than even he had anticipated. It was a glorious coupling, both un-
settling and complicated. This was life as he
wanted it.

CHAPTER NINE

FEELING LIKE THIS about Cesar resulted in clear thinking, forward planning, even sensible behaviour flying out of the window. The power of her feelings for him allowed for no modification or delay but, as always, once they reached the summit there was only one way down. Uncertainty beckoned.

They dressed quickly. She covered the evidence of outrageously good sex with a fast smoothing of her hair and a few deep, steadying breaths. Cesar made no adjustments. His hair remained as wild as ever, while his breathing had remained steady throughout. For him, sex was an exercise, probably not entirely dissimilar in his mind from the body-stretching workout they undertook on horseback in the ring. And now exercise time was over, and he was ready to move on.

That was how much it had meant to him.

Her mind was made up. There could be

no more self-indulgence. Incredible sex with someone who was starting to mean far too much to her was a luxury she couldn't afford. She had to find a way to curb want and replace it with enough confidence to make Cesar hear the truth.

She left first, striding ahead of him to the ranch house. She cared about the people there, and those currently staying in her retreat must be kept safe. Her feelings had to be put aside.

Loading her tray at the counter, she joined her brothers and Jess at a long table in the centre of the comfortably furnished wood-panelled room. There was a moment of readjustment by those of her brothers who weren't remotely on Sofia's side. Raffa and Xander exchanged glances before carrying on with their meal, heads down. They'd always been so easy together, and now she felt like an unwelcome stranger. Yes, they'd always teased her. That's what brothers did. But deep down they were there for her. Not any more, thanks to her supposed betrayal of them, and Cesar. She had to mend that rift before it became too wide to bridge.

Jess and Olivia were the only ones to greet her with genuine warmth, perhaps sensing there was more to Sofia's story than they knew. When Cesar had collected his food and joined them, there was another discernible rustle of interest around the table, but everyone was too cool to comment. He soon put them at ease with easy banter, culminating in, 'I'll take any seat.' Which just happened to be thigh to thigh with Sofia.

It was hard to breathe. How hard would it be to fall in love with him? She covered her concerns with a grin as she turned to Jess. 'Work us harder tomorrow.' Exhaustion might help. Something had to.

Jess winked, as if she understood everything. 'Don't worry, I intend to,' she promised.

'Good.' Cesar was the only one at the table who responded. Pushing his chair back, he stood up. 'We'll all benefit from another good workout tomorrow.' He glanced at Sofia. 'I'm going to take a sluice down in the yard.'

Sofia flicked a quick glance at Jess. It felt good to have an ally. She had no idea how much Jess knew, but she could feel her sympathy coming in waves across the table.

Was she expected to join him? Sofia wondered when Cesar paused at the door. Turning away, she continued her chat with Jess. They had a lot to talk about. They both had to put up with her brothers.

Her gaze strayed out of window. Cesar was tipping well water over his head. She clenched and unfurled her fingers, remembering how he'd felt beneath her hands.

Droplets of water went flying from his thick black hair when he shook his head like an angry wolf. His torso was gleaming and wet. How was she supposed to feel nothing for this man?

'Sofia?'

She turned to face Jess. 'I'm sorry... Forgive me. I was distracted.'

Jess grinned. 'Who wouldn't be? Anyway, I was just saying, prepare to be exhausted tomorrow. There's less than a month to go before the first match. These might be exhibition matches, but you know as well as I do that when your brothers and Cesar are playing against a rival like Nero Caracas, there's no such thing as a friendly game.'

Jess wasn't exaggerating. Nero and his team Assassin were their closest rivals. 'Work us hard. Give us every advantage you can. The rest is up to fate, and how we play on the day.'

Placing her hand over Sofia's, Jess gave it a squeeze as she whispered discreetly, 'I know how worried you are, but you don't need to worry about Cesar. He's overcome mountains before, and knows how to handle himself. Concentrate on looking after yourself.'

'Thank you.' *For being my friend* didn't need to be said.

Sofia glanced through the window at Cesar. Another lonely night beckoned, and then a new day with all that that entailed.

'Need a leg-up?'

She looked around to see Cesar standing behind her. Feelings swamped her.

'No, thanks. I can manage.'

'Please yourself.' With a shrug, he sprang into the saddle and cantered into the arena.

Jess placed Sofia behind Cesar in the line, which taunted Sofia with the sight of a back view as good as his front. Powerful and unyielding, Cesar's mighty shoulders and straight spine could have been a metaphor for the way he lived.

Her heart clenched at the thought of any harm coming to him during the matches. They would be rough, they would be hard; neither side would give way without a fight. And then there was the blackmailer she had to deal with, which was like coping with a virus, sneaky and unpredictable, working in the shadows to bring a victim down—

'Sofia, are you with us?' Jess was calling from across the ring. 'Change direction now!'

Sofia wheeled her pony around just in time to avoid a collision with Xander, who blasted her with a derisive look as he cantered past.

In the unlikely event that Cesar spares the time to actually hold a conversation with you, how likely is it that he'll jump at the chance to help you with your blackmailer?

She had to hope pretty high. Like her brothers, Cesar was a man of principle—

'Sofia!' Jess rode up alongside. 'Do you need to take a break?'

'No. Sorry. I'm on it.'

'I hope so. Carelessness leads to accidents at this level of training.'

'It won't happen again, Jess.'

Just as she would never, *ever* write another article. Now all she had to do was persuade Cesar of that, and that the original article had been so heavily doctored she'd hardly recognised it.

Well, that should be easy, she reflected as Cesar gave her a black look for reckless riding.

Easy or not, it had to be done.

Her chance came at the end of the afternoon session when everyone left to freshen up. Sofia's legs felt like wood. She couldn't remember working so hard on a horse, and for the first time in her memory she stumbled when she dismounted.

Cesar was at her side in an instant, steadying her with one hand firmly lodged beneath her arm. 'Too much for you? You made a bit of a mess of today's training. Maybe don't ask Jess to make things harder tomorrow?' he suggested dryly. 'Was there any particular reason behind your request to make things hard for you?'

She chose to ignore that question. 'Training's hard for all of us. I can take it.'

Cesar gave her a critical look. 'Can you?'

Ignoring that too, she focused on the one thing that mattered. 'I have to talk to you—and I mean talk. To clear the air,' she explained when Cesar remained silent.

'It will take more than a chat to do that.' He was already turning away. 'Barbecue this evening,' he announced.

'Cesar, please,' she insisted, grabbing a moment alone as soon as he'd finished spelling out the details. 'We can't go on like this, not if we hope to play well as a team.'

He stared at her hand on his arm. She stood back. Good enough for sex, she wasn't good enough for Cesar to engage in conversation apparently. Now she was mad. Which was unfortunate timing, as the stable hands had arrived to take charge of the ponies.

'If only you were so caring about your human counterparts,' Cesar observed, holding the door for her to pass through as they left the building.

She always spelled out her pony's preferences, and mentioned any worries she might have about the animal's condition after hard training.

Her heart lurched as their hands brushed. How was she ever going to concentrate when that was all it took? She had to. She must. She couldn't lose her brother, and she couldn't lose Cesar. 'There's something you need to know.'

'Sounds intriguing.' He speared her with a stare until it was hard to believe she had any secrets left.

'Can we talk now?'

He shrugged. 'I can spare you five minutes.'

She'd take it. 'Thanks.'

'Follow me—'

'No.' She shook her head. 'I need you to follow me.'

Without looking back to see if Cesar was following, she led the way to what had quickly become Sofia's favourite place on Cesar's ranch. It was a secluded spot by the river, where she could read and think, not that she got much spare time to do either. Her destination was a woodland grove where she could sit, sheltered by a copse of trees. It was an idyllic spot on the banks of a fast-flowing river, but it wasn't easy to reach, which was half of its attraction. Few made the effort, so it was completely private. Brambles on the ground threatened to trip unwary visitors, but for someone brought up in the country like Sofia, who was accustomed to trekking over difficult ground, it was a hidden treasure.

She could hear Cesar's long strides behind her. He had to hear her out, then he could send her home if he wanted to. Either way, she had to make a stand.

'My mother used to being me here,' Cesar revealed when they stood on the banks of the fast-flowing river. 'It was part of my introduction to a brighter world, she'd tell me. A world where things are clean, and clear, if you remain still and allow yourself to hear.'

Would he? Would he allow himself to hear? With all her heart, she hoped he would.

'When I was older, I'd come here on my own to think.'

'Did it help?' she asked, wanting to open this window onto Cesar's early life wide.

'Five minutes,' he reminded her, closing off. 'So you'd better be fast. What do you want to talk to me about?'

If that was the way he was going to play it, she'd be just as blunt. 'I'm being black-mailed.'

Obviously shocked, Cesar recovered fast. 'Go on,' he prompted.

'I signed up to write a light, fluffy piece for a fee I could plough into my retreat. At the time I had no idea Howard Blake was such an unscrupulous man, or that he would seize the opportunity to take my material and doctor it beyond all recognition. Now he's threatening to publish more articles under my name. I'm guessing they won't do you or my brothers any favours. I don't know why he's got it in for you. I do know my reputation will be ruined, but that's nothing in comparison to losing the love and trust of my brothers, and causing you more harm. If I could wind back the clock, and change things, I would, but...'

Cesar was staring out across the stream in silence. 'Did you hear me?'

'Every word.' he assured her.

She couldn't believe how calm he was, though alert like a wolf on point.

'Your five minutes are up.'

There was no warmth in his voice as he swung around to head back up the bank. 'But—'

'I promised you five minutes,' he said, briefly turning. 'You've had that and more.'

'But, please, I—'

'Don't,' Cesar warned quietly. 'How could the chance to see your by-line above an article in a national newspaper prove such a lure you were prepared to throw your brothers under a bus and me along with them?'

'Weren't you listening? It wasn't like that. Those weren't my words.'

'So you say. What I read was invented scandal. Maybe you dressed up the facts until they provided outrageous amounts of click bait with no basis of truth. How do I know? How can I be sure of you, Sofia? The dates on which your accusations were based were entirely accurate, but the events you wrote about never happened.'

'Because I didn't write them!' she exploded, growing increasingly frustrated. 'Believe me,

Cesar. Have I ever given you cause to doubt me before?'

'How well did I know you before?' he countered.

'Do you seriously believe I would hurt those I love—or, almost worse, those vulnerable individuals recovering at my retreat? If you think so little of me, I'm wasting my time.'

'Maybe you are,' he agreed.

'I need help,' she admitted grimly as she clambered up the bank to join him. 'What started out as what I thought was a normal relationship between an enthusiastic amateur journalist and a newspaper mogul quickly turned sour. If Blake can do that to me and get away with it, how many more people are at risk? He has to be stopped, and I can't do this on my own.'

There was a silence she thought would never end, and then Cesar said the words she had hoped and prayed he would. 'This is not something you can handle on your own,' he agreed. 'I know Blake from our schooldays together. We attended the same boarding school. He was the class bully, picking on younger boys with no one to defend them.'

'So you defended them,' she said.

A grim smile firmed Cesar's lips as he thought back. 'It was a full-time occupation.'

'And one he never forgave you for,' she guessed.

Cesar nodded briefly. 'Blake was the type to bear grudges. I always suspected him of being behind the swindler who tried to steal the throne by cosying up to my mother. There have been numerous attacks over the years.'

'Of which I'm just the latest?'

'Don't beat yourself up,' Cesar said, to her surprise. 'You couldn't know how devious he was, or how he would use you to get at me.'

Hope surged through her. 'So you believe me?'

'I'm giving you the benefit of the doubt,' Cesar prevaricated.

'I handed him ammunition on a plate.'

'To help your retreat.'

'Yes.' Still reeling from the thought that Cesar might believe her, and that he might help after all, she asked the obvious question. 'Why have you never hit back at him before?'

'Make myself as small as him?' Cesar

shook his head. 'There are other, more efficient ways to deal with a bully like Blake, subtle ways that will keep him in a moral cage.'

CHAPTER TEN

CURIOUS TO HEAR MORE, Sofia continued with her explanation. 'To start with, it seemed as if fate had dropped an opportunity into my hand. 'Writing "a piece of fluff" for the features page was how Lord Blake put it. It seemed such a good opportunity to bring in much-needed money to support the expansion of my retreat.'

'Easy money?' Cesar challenged. 'There's no such thing. You should have been suspicious right away.'

'It's easy to be wise in retrospect,' Sofia argued, 'but when you've spent months casting about for ways to keep things running, you're open to any idea that seems remotely feasible.'

'Writing an article exposing the antics of the super-rich seemed feasible to you?'

'That wasn't how I phrased it. There was no mention of "super-rich". I wrote about humorous incidents that happened on the world tour. None of them were scandalous or libellous. I certainly didn't depict you as an "elitist degenerate", which was one of the descriptions used. What I wrote made you and my brothers seem approachable. It was supposed to make people laugh, not cause trouble.'

'Blake couldn't have doctored the piece without your ready supply of facts,' Cesar pointed out.

'But that's just it. Some of those facts I didn't even know. How could I? I don't have access to your diary. So now do you see why I need your help?'

As Cesar's thoughtful gaze rested on her face, she felt a great sense of weariness at her seemingly endless attempts to try to explain what had happened. Why wouldn't he take her at her word? She'd never knowingly told a lie, and had believed that as soon as she opened up, Cesar would believe her.

It didn't take much for weariness to turn into anger. Staring at Cesar's back as he made his way home was the final straw. Catching up, she stood grim-faced in his way. 'At least have the courtesy to let me know what you think.'

Lifting her aside, he moved on.

'I expect a fair hearing, and all I get is ignored? How do you expect anyone to stop Howard Blake if you turn your back and walk away?'

'I'm not ignoring you, but this is not the time,' he said, striding on.

'Not the time?' She caught up. 'What do you mean? What else is going on?'

At least he stopped walking.

'You're the only person I know who wields as much power as Howard Blake,' she pressed. 'Maybe more. Definitely more. If anyone can stop him, you can. Cesar, if your back was to the wall, wouldn't you do anything to make things right?'

'I've never been in that position.'

'I'm glad, but please have sympathy for those who aren't so lucky. I have to believe you can stop Blake hurting anyone else.'

She was puzzled when he didn't answer. 'Is there something you're not telling me?'

'It was a very different situation. A member of my family was under attack.'

Lifting her chin, she braced herself and ignored the sting. 'Family loyalty is paramount to me too, which is why I would never intentionally hurt my brothers. Blake will dig and dig until he finds something to use. He has to be stopped. You must be thinking I've got a cheek, asking you for help, but who else can I turn to?'

'Your brothers?' Cesar suggested in a dead tone.

'I've always wanted to stand on my own two feet. I caused this problem, so it's up to me to sort it out.'

'But you're asking for my help,' he pointed out impatiently. 'I don't see the difference.'

'You have a certain reputation when it comes to dealing with difficult people. Didn't you mention subtlety? I'm calling on your expertise.'

'Save your flattery.'

'I'll stop at nothing to prevent Howard Blake causing any more trouble. If I involve my brothers and they bring in the weight of the Acosta lawyers, this could run and run, doing more harm than good. I'm trying to avoid that.'

'You must have a record of the original article on your computer to prove that it was changed?'

'Conveniently, my computer was stolen when burglars targeted my home.'

'Stolen from your retreat?'

'Yes.'

'Do you vet the people you allow in? Your brothers tell me there's very little security.'

'That was the whole point. I wanted people to feel free, not trapped.'

'Oh, Sofia, Sofia.' Cesar gave her a long, considering look. 'I'm beginning to think that you tried to do your best—'

'If you're going to be patronising—'

'Stop,' he commanded.

She tensed at the touch of his hand on her arm.

'Sometimes a warm heart can put you at a disadvantage.'

Cesar's tone was gentle, but she had no intention of being treated like a child. Bringing Howard Blake down would take both of them equally.

Giving herself a moment, she refocused her mind. This wasn't about pride or personal considerations, but getting a job done. 'How did you stop him last time?' she asked briskly, turning to stare Cesar in the eyes.

'Money talks?' He sounded faintly amused, as if he had accepted both her stand and the fact that massive wealth could be useful in a number of ways. 'My last run-in with Blake involved a member of my family, someone else with a kind heart, falling into Blake's clutches. It was necessary to step in to protect that family member.'

'Your mother?' Sofia guessed.

Cesar was too protective and too discreet to answer her question, both of which counted in his favour.

'Howard Blake was silenced, and that's all you need to know. He got to keep his publishing empire in a deal that suited us both.'

It was hard to imagine Blake, a man who had bullied and hectored *her*, turning over meekly, though coming up against Cesar would be daunting, she imagined, even for a man as unscrupulous as Howard Blake. Her brother Xander had once referred to Cesar as being the most resourceful and determined individual he'd ever met, adding that Cesar always protected those who needed him. 'I never thought I was Blake's first target, and I'm sure I won't be the last. I'm strong enough to take the consequences, but what about the next person he picks on?'

'So what's your plan?'

'From what you've told me, and from personal experience, we know Blake can't stop himself targeting those weaker than himself. It's like an addiction. You've already dealt with him successfully, and I'm lucky to have you onside. I do have you onside?' She went on before Cesar had a chance to answer. 'We can't hang his future targets out to dry. We can't turn our backs. We have to stop him. Someone has to bring him to account.'

'You?' Cesar interrupted with a cynical lift of his brow.

'I can't do this without your help,' she said honestly.

'So you propose co-operation between us?'

'Is that so bad?'

Sofia's voice was quiet and intense. Her stare remained fixed on his face. How could he remain unsympathetic when Blake had targeted both his mother and his sister? His mother had taken a lover, a conman planted by Blake, he now thought, and there was a sex tape featuring Olivia. These were Blake's weapons of choice. Rage roared inside him as he recognised Sofia as an equally attractive target for a bully. Desperate to keep the retreat that meant so much to her going at any cost, she was exactly the type of victim Howard Blake loved to prey on. Sofia must have been a prized victim, giving Blake direct access to the Acosta brothers and his old enemy Cesar. How he must have gloated, thinking he could send them all down like a line of dominoes.

'Cesar?'

Fury must have been written on his face. Most would shrink from it, but not Sofia. She stood to confront him and barred his way. 'We'll call him out,' she said fiercely.

He raised a brow. 'How do you propose to do that?'

'We'll set a trap. We'll feed him false information and then expose it as a lie.'

'He'll see that coming a mile off,' he reflected out loud. 'The confrontation has to be face to face. So I'll deal with him.' He held up his hand when she started to argue. 'I don't want you anywhere near him. This is something I will handle alone.'

Even as he was speaking, an idea was niggling at his brain. There was no time to waste. He had investigations to make. 'Is that it?'

Sofia reached out a hand as if to stop him, but then she withdrew it and lowered her gaze in a way that made her seem suddenly fragile. 'You go on,' she said. 'I'd like to stay here for a while.'

'Be back before dark. Remember the Apennine wolves. They roam freely in the forest.'

'I won't forget. I can look after myself. Remember?'

She stared up, her eyes luminous and unblinking. He didn't move. He couldn't move. How could he leave her alone in the forest? The light was fading, and there was more than one wolf on the prowl. Sofia had made a dangerous enemy in Howard Blake, and Cesar would take no chances. 'You're coming with me so I know that you're safe.'

'A few minutes ago you'd have liked to throw me in the stream,' she commented with amusement.

'Never,' he assured her. 'I'd only have to jump in and save you.'

'I'd save myself,' she insisted, lifting her chin.

'And how would you do that?'

'I'd do it somehow,' she assured him stubbornly.

Somehow wouldn't help her with Howard Blake. 'I do need you to do something for me,' he revealed as they started to walk back.

'Tell me.'

'The best way to show Blake he can't hurt you, let alone destroy your brothers and me, as he seems to think he can, is by making sure we win those matches and raise more money than even Howard Blake can dream of for our charities.'

'You're cutting me out,' she said with affront, having read the subtext behind his words. 'You can't do this alone. Cesar—what are you going to do?'

'It's better that you don't know. That no one knows.'

'Don't you trust me?'

She was hurt when he didn't answer right away, but his mind was made up. Keeping

Sofia safe, saving her brothers and even a country from the spite of Howard Blake, was more important than explanations. 'Be the best you can be,' he advised. 'That's your revenge when it comes to Howard Blake.'

There were tears in her eyes, he realised when he turned to look at Sofia. She had guts but a tender underbelly, reminding him that emotions did matter, whether he liked it or not. 'Don't worry about Blake. I'll deal with him, so he never hurts anyone else. And when this is over,' he added in an attempt to turn her mind from the dark side to something lighter, 'I'll commission a portrait of the winning team.'

For a moment he thought his offer had missed the mark. In fairness, contemplating the evil of a man like Blake then switching to the prospect of the quiet contemplation involved when Sofia picked up her brush and paints was quite a stretch, but one Sofia had to make if she was ever to sleep easily again.

He should have known she was equal to the task.

'The winning team had better not be Nero Caracas and the Assassins,' she said, smiling in a way that touched him somewhere deep. 'I don't have enough black paint.'

It had been good to walk back to the ranch house with Cesar with some ease at last between them. It made her hopeful that other things could change for the better.

But now, back in her room, without the beauty of the countryside surrounding her, she had started to worry again—primarily about Cesar. His promise to 'handle things'. What did that mean? If Cesar could deal with Howard Blake help without putting himself at risk, that was one thing, but she had never intended him to do this on his own.

Getting ready for dinner involved showering before changing into clean jeans and a casual top for the promised barbecue. Staring at her reflection in the mirror above the sink, she craved the chance for them to continue getting to know each other outside sex. They'd made a small start down by the river, but would he take things further? It took two to form a relationship, and Cesar's wishes were one thing determination alone couldn't influence.

Cesar hosted the barbecue. He got on so well with her brothers. Jess and Olivia came straight over to welcome her. 'Okay?' Jess asked. 'Nothing aching too much?'

Only my heart, she thought, smiling. 'I'm fine.'

Olivia came up with some startling news. 'I've seen the looks that pass between you and my brother. Jess and I have been talking, and you don't need to tell us that Howard Blake set you up. Jess knows everything about my run-in with Blake, so if you need allies, look no further.'

'Thank you.'

'Take my advice,' Olivia continued. 'First find the mole.'

'The mole?' Sofia frowned.

'Someone filmed me secretly. I don't know if you heard about the tape?' Olivia pressed. 'Anyway, it was explicit,' she continued, sparing Sofia the need to answer, 'and somehow it found its way to Howard Blake. That someone is almost certainly the same person who supplied the dates and details you couldn't. Someone helped Blake doctor that article.

I know it wasn't you, and it most certainly wasn't me.'

An unseen enemy was one to fear the most. Fear tightened around Sofia's heart. She drew a deep breath, and pushed it aside. 'Do you have any suspects in mind?'

'I do,' Olivia confirmed, 'but I can't prove anything yet. We'll speak again,' she promised.

Sofia's mind was spinning as Olivia moved away. Cesar's sister had left her with more questions than answers. Cesar's bottomless resources would open many doors, but now Sofia wished she hadn't asked him for help. The thought of putting Cesar in danger was the worst nightmare imaginable. She had to put things right. Quite how she was going to do that, she had no idea yet. Olivia only proved that caution must be her watchword.

'I thought it was me you wanted to talk to, not my sister,' Cesar remarked dryly as he loaded Sofia's plate with food.

'Steady. Am I not allowed to speak to your sister? No more food,' she insisted, laughing as he continued to stack it on her plate. 'You're not feeding my brothers.'

'I'll take your plate to the table,' he offered.

Everyone else was seated by the time they arrived. Sofia sat on a bench facing her brothers, while Cesar straddled the end of it, so he was facing her.

'Olivia is a hothead,' he informed her. 'Don't believe everything she says.'

'Even if what Olivia says makes sense?' Sofia queried.

Cesar shrugged. 'Just don't allow her to draw you into one of her ill-thought-out schemes.'

'What makes you think I don't have schemes of my own?'

'If you do, I must insist you run them past me first.'

She almost choked on her burger. Chugging down a glass of water, she shook her head. 'I can't believe you sometimes. You mentioned co-operation? I get that. Putting safeguards in place is only sensible, but to defer to you on every decision I make?'

'I'm trying to keep you safe, Sofia.'

'And I'm trying to keep you safe,' she reminded him. Glancing around, she tried to work out who the mole might be. Each group was an island separate from the rest, but could any of them be guilty of betraying Cesar's trust? It seemed unlikely.

'I have a lot of things to put right and I don't expect you, or anyone else, to do that for me,' she stated firmly. 'I may not have your seemingly limitless resources, but neither am I incapable.'

'Or as experienced as me at dealing with sharks like Howard Blake,' Cesar pointed out.

'I'm a fast learner.'

'Fast learners listen to advice.'

Sitting back, she closed her eyes briefly. 'Do you have any idea how annoying you can be?'

Cesar flashed a quick and, oh, so welcome smile. 'Some.'

'Well, just forget I said anything. I shouldn't have asked you for help.'

'That's a matter of opinion. Howard Blake is a slippery character.'

'All the more reason to stop him.'

'But not on your own.' Cesar articulated each word in a low, fierce tone.

With a laugh she pushed her plate away. 'Anyone would think you care.'

'I do care,' Cesar insisted, surprising her, but just as happy surprise leapt onto her face he added, 'I'm not looking for more tangles to unpick before the match. The clock is ticking. None of us can afford to be distracted. You expected something more?' he enquired, when she couldn't hide her shock.

Recovering fast, she said coolly, 'Why would I?'

'We can't talk here,' Cesar said, frowning. 'It's too noisy. My study...' He stood.

She'd seen his study. Desk. Floor. Rug. Hard chairs. Easy chairs. Inviting sofas. All options open. But to persuade Cesar not to do anything that might put him danger, was this the best chance she'd get?

CHAPTER ELEVEN

LEAVING THE TABLE, she joined Cesar as they walked the short distance to the ranch house. Once inside they went straight to Cesar's study, where he directed her to an easy chair. He remained standing with his hip propped against the desk. 'So talk,' he invited.

'I've got nothing new to say. I just don't want you doing anything on my behalf that puts you in danger.'

'How much of your own money have you put into your retreat?'

'Every penny. And I mortgaged the property,' she admitted. 'I had to so I could take on more people.'

Cesar's look grew cynical. 'Were you planning to write more articles to fund this expansion?'

'No! Of course not! How can you even think that?'

'I'm curious as to how you intended to support yourself going forward.'

'I thought selling my paintings might help.' That sounded so lame now. How did she know anyone would buy them? So far she'd had a commission from her brother and the sniff of a promise from Cesar. That wouldn't be enough to support her retreat.

'How much do you need?' Cesar asked bluntly.

'I don't want a loan,' she said. 'I'll find the money.'

'You have a money tree?'

'I'll listen to any suggestions you care to make, but I won't sit on my hands while you go into battle on my behalf.'

'It's time to accept that you can't carry the world on your shoulders. I'm sure your brothers would be only too eager to help you if you didn't push them away.'

'I haven't pushed them away. It takes them all their time to speak to me.'

There was silence for a while and then Cesar reflected, 'I guess it must have been hard as a teenager in a household of overprotective brothers.'

'You have no idea,' she agreed, relaxing enough to smile as she thought back.

'I think I do,' Cesar argued. 'My sister was left without a father, and when my mother recovered from her grief she was…distracted, shall we say? I was in the Special Forces, and it was only when Olivia alerted me to trouble—and, believe me, Olivia seeks help from no one—that I left the army to save the throne from an unscrupulous man. So I'm not exactly out of practice when it comes to dealing with problems. I'd go as far as to say I'm your best hope.'

Maybe her only hope. 'Okay, but we do this together or not at all.'

'Too many chiefs,' Cesar cautioned.'

'You're not suggesting I leave it all to you?'

'It's not a suggestion,' he assured her.

'Not my way either,' she said, firming her jaw.

Cesar went to stare out of the window. 'My mother grieved long and hard for my father,' he said without turning around. 'Years passed and then she took a lover. Howard Blake's press were all over it. I was still in the army when the palace made an announcement that this man from nowhere, no history, no relatives, no obvious experience to make him a suitable candidate to support the Queen in her duties, planned to join her on the throne.'

'As your mother's equal?' Sofia asked with surprise. 'I didn't realise it went that far.' The throne should rightfully pass to Cesar, and she could only imagine how he must have felt, or how delicately he'd had to handle the situation without upsetting his mother, who must have been very vulnerable at the time. That, as well as protecting Olivia from a scandal, made her wonder if Cesar ever spared a thought for himself.

'What's your plan?' he asked as he swung around.

She didn't want to talk about herself, or what *she* was going to do. She wanted to talk about Cesar so she could try to understand this deep and complex man. In short order, Cesar had lost his father, found himself head of a prominent family, and been thrown into the turmoil of fixing his mother and sister's lives. He could only do that by pushing his feelings aside. Joining the Special Forces might have given the wild youth an anchor, but he'd been forced to give that up. Cesar's recent life seemed to have been one of constant sacrifice, and now she was throwing up yet another hurdle.

She understood his mother's reasons. Grief could throw anyone off kilter. Sofia had always tried to live up to what she believed were her dead parents' expectations of her, but this time, like the Queen, she'd gone too far. If she'd called a halt when she'd built a small retreat with limited places, none of this would have happened. But so many had applied to go there. How could she choose who could stay and who to turn away?

'So what next, Sofia?'

Cesar was waiting for her answer. He had the world on his shoulders already, and now he expected her to load him down with more.

'Sofia?' he pressed.

'I plan to turn my fledgling investigative skills on Howard Blake,' she revealed.

'Hoping he has an Achilles heel?' Cesar guessed.

'I have to hope so,' she confessed. 'But it's more than that. I want to understand his jealousy towards you and the way he'll stop at nothing to destroy you, even using me.'

'I can't argue with that,' Cesar admitted. 'I've thought the same thing myself.'

'So we do agree on something?' she said wryly, hoping she was right.

When Cesar didn't answer, she decided it was time for bed. Getting up from her chair, she said, 'If I do find out anything else that might be helpful, I'll let you know.'

'You do that,' Cesar agreed. 'Goodnight, Sofia.'

'Goodnight.'

He didn't call her back or come after her. And, of course, she was glad about that.

Was she?

The sound of the door closing behind Sofia rang in Cesar's ears for some time. Not that she was angry, or even disappointed he hadn't pulled a rabbit out of a hat to show her when it came to his plans for Howard Blake. When he did decide what to do, he'd be the only one with that information. It was safer that way.

External influences hadn't made Sofia leave in such a hurry, he concluded, but the pull between them had done the damage. They'd shared a look. She'd moistened her lips. Her cheeks had flushed pink and her breathing quickened, but instead of taking things further he'd made it clear that wasn't going to happen, at which point she'd left the room. Sex was the answer to a lot of things, but not this.

Exhaling a long, steady breath, he sat back. What was this woman doing to him? When things looked as if they might become complicated by feelings, he always pulled back. Capable of feeling the deepest emotion, he also knew how to hide it well, thanks to understanding the cost of love. He had idolised his father, the strongest and noblest of men, but still found it hard to accept that a fall from a horse during training could have brought such a well-lived life to a sudden and unalterable end.

He and his father were the same in that they solved problems and found solutions. His father's tragic death was the first time Cesar had been faced by a catastrophe he could neither change nor soften. The end of one way of living and the beginning of another, quite different life had been brutal. One minute his father had been laughing and joking, poised and confident as he'd cantered around the arena, and the next his horse had stumbled, throwing him over its head. And that was it. The end. Over. Never to move, breathe, speak, or offer loving advice again.

Everything had changed on that day. His mother had been hysterical, his sister numb with shock. From a confident, hard-living youth, home on furlough from the army, he had been catapulted into a world where caring for people was more important than crowns. Stability for family and country had become his guiding light from that moment on, just as personal feelings had become a complete and utter irrelevance. All that mattered had been putting things back on an even keel.

The bombshell of the King's death had spread a shroud of fear across the citizens of Ardente Sestieri as people had wondered what would come next. Prince Cesar, the wild youth whose exploits had entertained them, was surely not fit to be King? Cesar's lifestyle hadn't mattered to his people when his father had been alive, but for such a solid and reliable presence on the throne to be replaced by someone unknown had taken a lot a lot of living down. The trust he'd won since then could be lost in a heartbeat.

At one point he'd wondered how his mother would survive the loss of his father. They had been two sides of the same coin. How would that one, lonely side of the coin weather the wear and tear of ruling, with only one face, one opinion, one decision-maker to hold the reins, with no one to advise, curb or recommend? His mother had needed him to step up, and he'd answered her call gladly. With her so-called suitor dismissed, the Queen would rule alone with Cesar as her chief advisor. Nothing must stand in the way of that.

It was in everyone's interest to bring Howard Blake to account. But there was another reason. Sofia had shown him her vulnerable side. He couldn't walk away from that. This was a time to keep her close. He had to, if he was to keep her safe.

What other reason could there be?

Pushing his chair back, he left his study to track her down.

* * *

He found her in the empty stable where she had gone to sort out her thoughts. Whatever else was going on in her life, animals always soothed her. Cesar lost no time in delivering his broadside. 'I can't let you approach Howard Blake on your own. I won't allow it!'

Brain and body moved as one for Cesar, and he was in front of her in a heartbeat. Scrambling to her feet, she faced him down. 'Cesar—'

'Yes, Cesar!' he cut across her. 'Who the hell else do you think would chase you down to stop you walking blindfold into danger?'

He really cared? She could see the concern in his eyes. How did she feel about that? Thrilled. Surprised. And also keenly aware that Cesar's concern could stand in the way of her setting things right.

'I'm glad you came,' she said, quickly marshalling her thoughts. 'I wanted to let you know what I've done so far.'

'What you've done?' Far from this enticing him to back off, Cesar's expression was thunderous. 'Without telling me first?'

'My plans are still in the very early stages,'

she explained in what she hoped was a soothing tone. 'I won't need an army or strong-arm
tactics—'

'Just tell me what you've done,' Cesar bit
out.

'I just made a call.'

'Who did you call?' She'd never seen him
like this. She could only describe it as an-
guished. 'Tell me what you've done, Sofia.
I hope you haven't put yourself in danger?'

'I called a woman who lives at my retreat,
the same woman who passed on the original
request from Howard Blake for me to write
an article. I trusted her. Dante always says I
trust everyone too quickly. Now I must face
the possibility that Dante's right, and this
woman and Howard might be in league.'

Cesar frowned. 'But how would she know
the dates in my diary?'

'Maybe there's more than one conspirator,'
Sofia allowed. 'Howard Blake's pockets are
deep enough to hire an army of moles. All
I offer is a haven until people are ready to
face the world again, while he offers a lot
of money. Who could blame her if she was
tempted?'

'I could,' Cesar said coldly. 'You're far too soft, Sofia.'

'I'm not soft at all,' she argued, 'but I do know what it's like to feel you've no control over your life, and to wonder and fear what's coming next. Seizing back even a little bit of control in those circumstances feels good.'

Cesar dismissed this with an impatient huff. 'You credit the person who quite possibly betrayed you with finer feelings than they deserve. If you have a suspect you should let me follow it up. I have the resources,' he pointed out. 'And whatever our differences, I would never allow someone to harm you and get away with it.'

'But you have enough to do.' Having asked Cesar for help, she was having second thoughts. He did have enough to do, and she had only made things harder.

'You don't know what you're up against,' he said with an impatient gesture.

'But I do, and I also have a theory as to why this is escalating. Jealousy,' she declared. 'I know it makes no sense when Blake's as rich as Croesus, but for some people even too much is never enough.'

Cesar didn't argue, but holding his stare for any length of time was never a good idea. Her body was always ready to seize the smallest cue, and this was not the right time to do that. This felt like the first time they'd ever talked, really talked, and both of them had listened. Surely that was something worth preserving and treasuring? All she'd wanted had been to build the connection between them and hopefully watch it turn into something deeper and more meaningful. Yes, her body burned to feel his touch again, nothing had changed where that was concerned, but now her heart yearned for company.

'You will not do this on your own. Understood?'

Cesar's instruction jolted her out of gentler thoughts. 'Don't forget I survived a house full of brothers,' she reminded him.

'Howard Blake is nothing like your brothers, and I shouldn't need to tell you that.'

'You don't,' she said, 'but if you think I'm going to sit on my butt, doing nothing, you're wrong. You have a country to consider, as well as a mother and sister to protect. Your duty lies there. I got into this mess, and now I'm going to get out of it.'

'I won't release you from your training,' Cesar told her with a closing gesture of his hands.

He wasn't used to being countermanded, let alone be taken out of the game, but Sofia was in no mood to give ground. 'You can't stop me,' she said. 'We're here because we choose to be here, not because you commanded our attendance. All of us are successful in our own right—some more successful than others,' she conceded with a shrug, 'but seriously, Cesar, you can leave this to me.'

'Seriously, Sofia,' he mocked with venom, 'that will never happen, so put it out of your mind.'

He swung her round so fast the air was sucked from her lungs. The time for calm reason had gone. 'Do you seriously think I'll allow you to risk your life? Don't you realise there's a kingdom at stake and that's what he's after? Blake tried once with my mother, dangling a gigolo in front of her. Do you think he'd care what happens to you? You'll be collateral damage—just another counter for

Blake to play and discard when it suits him. I won't allow you to do that—for your sake, and for the sake of everyone who cares about you. Your life is worth nothing to Howard Blake. *Nothing!* Don't you get it?'

Cesar's face was very close. His eyes scorched hers. She'd never seen so much passion in one man. Perhaps because Cesar never showed emotion it seemed all the greater now. Whatever it was she felt, it was not the urge to pull away or even to stand on tiptoe to give him a kiss—*definitely not that*. What she felt, deep down, through every fibre of her being was the urge to reassure him. Cesar had been through enough. 'I'm not your responsibility, and I promise I won't get hurt. I'll be back to play in the matches before you know it. And we'll win—in every way there is,' she added with icy resolve.

He couldn't believe what he was hearing, and frankly he'd had enough. Sofia appeared convinced that fairy-tales could come true and that good would prevail over evil. She refused to see the danger. Whatever he said fell would fall on deaf ears. Fortunately, he'd cut his teeth on an equally wilful sister so he was in familiar territory. 'I'll bar you from leaving the kingdom if I have to. I'm not joking, Sofia.'

But the sterner his tone, the brighter grew the gleam of amusement in Sofia's eyes. 'What's wrong with you?' he demanded. But he knew. He'd seen the same thing on the battlefield. In a hazardous situation humour often showed itself, as if to thumb its nose at danger. That was the case here. Sofia thought she knew the person she was dealing with, but he really knew.

'Whatever it takes,' he warned as he took hold of her arms. His mouth was so close to hers now they shared the same breath, the same air. Her eyes held challenge, and however much he glowered back she smiled at him, until the laugh she'd been smothering broke free. 'You think this is funny?' he demanded. 'Or are you addicted to playing with fire?'

Her expression changed. Her eyes filled with an expression he rejected, not need or passion—compassion. 'Stop looking at me like that,' he warned.

'Someone should,' she said coolly.

'What are you talking about?' Letting her go, he stood back.

'It must be lonely in your ivory tower. I was hoping I could pay a visit and get to know you.'

'Isn't that what we've been doing?'

She slowly shook her head. 'So far you've lectured me and I've listened, but now I'm going to tell you what I'm doing next.'

'You think?' he scoffed.

When reason failed, his instinct took over.

CHAPTER TWELVE

As CESAR DROVE his mouth down on hers, she knew that if there hadn't been so much pent-up longing inside her she would have... *What? Pushed him away?*

Not a chance. Caring and hunger mixed in one fiercely compassionate need to be close to him. Pulling his head back, he stared down and smiled. 'Must you always choose a stable for your amorous encounters?'

'I didn't invite you to join me,' she countered, challenge firing in her eyes.

'Didn't you?' Cesar queried as he smoothly dispensed with her clothes. He was in even more of a hurry than she was, and she was desperate for release. Every part of her ached for him and rejoiced when he lifted her so she could lock her legs around his waist. Breath escaped her lungs in a long-drawn-out sigh as he plunged deep.

'Excellent,' Cesar growled, throwing his

head back in ecstasy as he slammed her against the wall.

Ripping his top out of the waistband of his jeans, she rested her face against his hard, warm chest and made a comment of her own.

'Your wish is my command,' Cesar informed her, losing no time before thrusting her screaming and bucking with pleasure into the abyss.

Grinding her fingers into his buttocks, she urged him on.

'Good?' he asked much, much later when she was quiet again.

She smiled up. 'What do you think?'

'Once is never enough?'

She laughed. Cesar had made her greedy. 'I swear, if you stop now, tease me, or make me wait, I'll—'

'You'll what?' he demanded in a low growl.

Nuzzling her neck, he whispered encouragement in his own language, which stole what little control she had left. 'Yes! *Yes!*' she begged, as breath shot out of her when Cesar plunged deep.

One powerful release stormed into the next. Rotating his hips made her more sensitive that she could ever have believed. Speech was impossible. Breathing was hard. Fractured shrieks of enjoyment was the best she could manage, while Cesar made sure he held her where he wanted her.

'I can't hold on,' she wailed at one point.

'You're not supposed to,' he said as he encouraged her to work her hips to the same greedy rhythm as his. 'Wildcat!' he approved when she dug her fingers into his shoulders.

'Faster! Harder!' Would she ever get enough?

The next climax came out of nowhere. She was powerless to resist. It was bigger, and far sweeter in its intensity than anything that had gone before. It seemed like for ever before the pleasure waves subsided, and when they did she was as helpless as a kitten, resting limp in Cesar's arms.

'Don't tell me I've finally exhausted you,' he remarked wryly as he lowered her carefully to the floor.

'I doubt you could ever do that,' she admitted, feeling warm and safe as he wrapped her in his arms and dipped his head to brush tender kisses against her mouth. 'But was that just to calm me, so I'll do anything you say?'

'Calm?' he queried. 'Are you in a different realm from me?'

'Answer my question.'

He held out his hands...the same hands that had held her safe and pleasured her until she could think of nothing else. 'What more do you want me to say, Sofia?'

'Reassurance that I haven't fallen for some sort of charm offensive,' she said bluntly.

'Surely you're not that insecure.'

Who knew what they were until they were tested? she wondered. Since getting together with Cesar everything mattered so much to her, too much maybe.

'Just tell me this didn't happen because you threatened you'd do whatever it took to bring me into line?'

'I have needs, just like you,' he dismissed.

'That's not an answer. Is that all it is?'

'Should there be more?'

Holding her breath, she closed her eyes briefly. Cesar could shut himself off completely whenever she tried to get close. What gave her the belief that she could break through his impregnable shell?

'Of course there's more,' he stated as he

raised her chin to stare into her eyes. His hands remained resting on her shoulders. She was unused to tenderness. Her brothers' idea of affection involved a not-so-gentle pat, and it had been a long time since she'd felt the loving touch of her parents. Cesar had caught her unawares, and now it was too late to hide the tears in her eyes.

He seemed puzzled. 'Is it so hard to believe that someone outside your immediate family cares what happens to you?' he asked. 'Or that a man wants you as fiercely as I do?'

'At least you're honest,' she said as she pushed a smile through her tears.

'Always,' Cesar promised, but within a moment he was back to his unemotional self. 'Come on, it's time to go.'

Face facts. Apart from the mind-blowing sex, she didn't know him that well.

How could he prove to a woman as strong and yet as fragile as Sofia that he meant her no harm?

By doing something together that didn't involve sex.

Thanking his inner voice with a silent two-word curse, he returned his attention to Sofia.

'Something wrong?' she asked as he pressed his lips down in thought.

He was only surprised at the unexpected interruption from an inner voice that had lain quietly dormant for years. Maybe nothing had happened in that time that had required it to speak up, the thought occurred to him. 'Do you play chess?'

'Chess?' Looking at him as if he'd gone mad, Sofia smoothed her hair, which required plucking quite a bit of hay out of it. 'Yes, I play chess,' she confirmed. 'Is that relevant?'

He shrugged. 'I don't see why not. We could go back to the ranch house, grab some food and a couple of beers, then engage in the age-old game of strategy. I find it clears the mind.'

'And you think it might help me?' she asked, curbing a smile.

'I don't see why not. It always helps me to focus and think clearly.'

'Something I need?' she suggested.

'Something civilised,' he confirmed,

'Civilised?' Sofia exclaimed on a laugh.

'When I play chess with my brothers it's like all-out war. If they even come close to losing, there's always a possibility they might upend the board and storm out.'

His lips tugged with amusement as he pictured the scene. 'Sounds reasonable.'

'Not to me,' Sofia assured him good-humouredly. 'But if you promise to behave, I'm happy to give you a game.'

'Come with me,' he invited.

There was a chessboard in his study. The room was quiet and warm. He sat on one side of the chess table and Sofia sat on the other. He set out the pieces. 'Ready?'

'Are *you* ready?' she challenged, dark eyes blazing with a competitive light.

'Are you sure it isn't you who upends the board if you lose? Just checking,' he soothed when she shot him one of her looks.

Doing something together that didn't involve sex turned out to be harder than expected. Sofia was a smart and merciless chess player. He knew the moment she asked to play the black pieces that she'd go for fool's mate.

Foiling her plan, he sat back.

'Okay,' she conceded, viewing the board through narrowed eyes. 'You got me.'

'Not yet,' he admitted. 'But I will.'

Maybe it was the heat they had created between them, or the recent memory of what had happened in the stable, but he was finding it increasingly hard to concentrate. Had she intentionally picked up the bishop and stroked it? After touching the piece, should he commit her to that move?

To hell with chess! His groin had tightened to the point of pain.

Having completed her move, Sofia tapped her fingers on the table.

'Would you like to use a timer for each move?' he asked.

'No.' She angled her head to study him. 'I like it when you take your time.'

'Be careful what you wish for.'

'Oh, I am,' she assured him in a tone that led him to wonder at what point Sofia had decided that moistening her lips with the tip of her tongue might be a good idea.

'Are you deliberately trying to distract me?'

'What makes you say that?' Her eyes widened in an expression of pure innocence.

When she closed them again, perhaps to hide her amusement, he noticed how a fringe of black lashes cast a crescent shadow on the perfectly carved line of her cheekbone. Dragging his gaze away, he focused on the game. Too late, as it happened.

'Check,' she said crisply.

Leaving his seat, he turned away from the board to rub a hand across the back of his neck in an attitude of abject defeat. He allowed Sofia to bask in her triumph for all of two seconds and then, smiling faintly, he turned back.

Confident of triumph, Sofia was studying him when she should have been continuing to study the pieces. Leaning over, he moved his queen. 'Checkmate,' he said softly.

Sofia made a sound of disgust. 'Who's the fool now?' she exclaimed. 'Well played,' she offered sportingly.

'Do you want to play another game?'

'Best of three?' she suggested.

'I suggest we play something else.'

Electricity flashed between them. No words were needed. Linking their fingers, he led her through the silent house. They mounted the stairs to his bedroom—or, more accurately, they almost reached the first landing. Pausing to kiss her was his downfall—their downfall. One kiss led to another and then they were fighting to rid themselves of clothes.

'I promise myself that one day I'm going to have you in bed,' he growled as she reached for him.

'Pillows? Covers? The whole nine yards?' she suggested.

'Depend on it.'

He took her to the hilt in a single thrust. There was no finesse about this mating. It was wild and fierce, and deliciously intense. As if the more they gorged on each other, the more they needed. One question remained. Would they regain reason in time to continue with everyday life? It didn't seem likely right now. Their lives were complex. His was eaten up by duty and responsibility, while hers was eaten up by concern for others.

Did she ever lavish time on herself?

'Again!' she insisted.

'Hey,' he soothed. 'Remember what I said? Next time in bed.'

* * *

This was true intimacy, Sofia mused contentedly as she lay replete in Cesar's arms on his enormous bed. Had there ever been a more unselfish lover? She doubted it. Cesar was sleeping. She should be too. They had training in the morning. Or, rather, he did.

Slipping out of bed, she ran to the shower, freshened up, and then dressed while she was still half-damp. Speed was of the essence. But she couldn't leave without imprinting every moonlit inch of Cesar on her mind. Naked he was glorious. Clothed he was glorious. Sleeping he was beautiful and strong. There was no tension on his face now, no weight of the world resting on his shoulders. She felt a quite ridiculous urge to go back over to the bed to pull the covers over him and give him one last kiss. Until the next time, she promised herself. This wasn't goodbye, it was just a temporary break. She wouldn't risk waking him. She'd do anything to protect him. And she would.

Stopping by Cesar's study, she quickly scribbled a note. She'd be back in time for the match and would spend every spare minute she had in training. She didn't expect to have many spare minutes, but she didn't want Jess or the team worrying about her fitness level.

Turning at the front door, she gazed around the hall and up the staircase, then back into Cesar's study, all the different places where they'd made love and grown closer.

They had grown closer. Cesar was slowly changing from the cold individual she'd first met into a man who gave her everything she needed. Cold was no longer a word she could associate with him. Cesar was hot and funny and caring. They hadn't exactly shared words of love, but silent communication could be more effective than words. Actions certainly were, and action was in her immediate future.

Closing the front door noiselessly behind her, she drew on the closeness that had grown between them to buoy her up and convince her that this was the right thing to do. There had been many moments of trust between them and, whatever happened next, she would never forget this time with Cesar.

She'd called a cab to take her to the airport so she could fly home to Spain. When she arrived back at her retreat, she'd root out the

truth. Someone had to be liaising with Howard Blake. If she couldn't uncover the truth
in Spain, she'd fly to London and confront
Blake at his office.

Tears stung her eyes at the thought of parting from Cesar, but she had a mission to complete before they'd meet again.

The cab she'd requested was waiting at the
gate. She turned to look at the sleeping house
one last time before climbing into the back
of it. A few lights were beginning to show
in the windows of the ranch house as people
woke up, though the sun had only now crept
over the horizon. Dawn was breaking on a
new day. Cesar would wake to find her gone.
'Forgive me,' she whispered.

CHAPTER THIRTEEN

THE AIR RANG blue with curses, leaving no one in any doubt that Prince Cesar of Ardente Sestieri was beyond furious.

'Understandable, Your Royal Highness,' Dom placated as he bent to remove the newspaper from Cesar's desk.

'Leave it!' Cesar thundered. 'My apologies,' he added grimly. 'This is not your fault.'

With a brief nod of acknowledgement at a rare climb-down by the Prince, Dom made himself scarce at the back of the room.

And still his presence continued to irritate Cesar. Maybe it was Dom's excessively obsequious behaviour lately. Royalty had staff. That was a given. Trusted staff were party to every aspect of Cesar's life. It was a boon he never took for granted, though right now he wished himself back in the army where he could trust his comrades with his life, and where he could take out his frustration on a daily basis with mind- and body-stretching exercises, without anyone knowing what he was thinking.

'The article is...upsetting,' Dom ventured from the shadows.

'You think that piece of garbage upset me?' he asked his aide with incredulity.

Snatching up the tabloid, he flung it down again in disgust. He'd skim-read the article that claimed to have been written by Sofia Acosta. In her spare time, presumably, which he happened to know had been non-existent. Blake had gone too far this time. But where the hell was she? It was Sofia's absence that was sending him into a rage. Concern for her that made his blood boil. The article was nothing more than a scurrilous piece of filth that he refused to dignify with a comment.

Why had she left without telling him where she was going? Why hadn't she woken him?

'It's hard to believe Signorina Acosta would write something like this,' Dom murmured at a level where he had to strain to hear him.

'Impossible,' he snapped.

Where was his control? What had happened to regal manners? All the niceties of life had deserted him around the same time as Sofia. As for the article, the author, whoever that might be, had gone for the jugular this time, crediting Cesar with a harem of imaginary lovers to rival the seraglio of Genghis Khan. It would take around three lifetimes for him to satisfy so many women. And, no, he refused to give it a try.

Whoever had written the article had stepped well over the line, insinuating that his relationship with Sofia was nothing more than a ruse planned by Sofia to ensnare him. She would never write such trash. The florid tone employed in the article was enough to clear her of guilt. No, this had come from the pen of some evil fantasist with a grudge and expensive tastes. The claims were so ridiculous they suggested that whoever was behind the plot to discredit him was fast becoming desperate.

'File a flight plan to Spain,' he instructed Dom. 'I'm leaving today.'

'In the middle of training?' Dom enquired with surprise.

'I'll be back before you know it.' The man

was really starting to annoy him. Dom had never questioned Cesar's decisions before.

'But the newspaper owner lives in Mayfair,' Dom pointed out, staring at him keenly.

'He's next on my list.'

'May I ask who's first?'

'No,' he said flatly. He'd had enough of Dom's intrusive change of manner. 'You may not.'

'Okay. Hand it over,' Sofia demanded as she took in the scene in the ranch house kitchen.

Cesar's aide, Domenico de Sufriente, was seated at the table, pounding his laptop, and leapt up guiltily when she walked into the room. He must have been confident she was on her way home. In fact, the cab ride to the airport had been long enough to figure out that there was another possible leak for Sofia to investigate, and that it was much closer to home.

Drawing himself up with affront, Dom pursed his mouth 'Hand over what, may I ask?'

'Your laptop,' Sofia said briskly.

'I beg your pardon?' Straightening his tie,

Cesar's equerry laughed, and it was a mean, sarcastic little laugh, Sofia registered. 'I don't think so,' he sneered.

As he was standing, she took her chance to glance at the screen. 'Howard Blake?' she queried, heart pounding as her suspicions were confirmed. 'You're sending an email to Howard Blake?' She pretended incomprehension. 'What on earth for? What can you possibly have to say to him? Were you perhaps warning him that I was on my way?'

'Is it customary where you come from to read people's mail?' he enquired cuttingly.

'I don't think I've ever done so before,' she admitted, 'and if you've nothing to hide, I can't see why you're making such a fuss.'

'Why should I have anything to hide?' Dom asked defensively as he slammed the lid of his laptop down. 'Your imagination has got the better of you. Personally, I'm surprised you've got the nerve to come back after the trash you've written about Prince Cesar.'

'Those were not my words, as you well know.' Dom's reddening cheeks suggested she'd caught him out. 'I wrote one article, which was changed completely. I'm not a career journalist. I'm a rider and a painter and a—'

'Philanthropist?' Dom suggested with an evil snigger, as if no one had any right to be kind to people, least of all Sofia.

'If you're referring to my retreat, it helps those who need it, and that's all I care about. You can deride it all you like, but you won't destroy it. I won't allow you to.'

'You think I'd waste my energy on destroying your pathetic little retreat?'

Judging by his expression, the only thing Dom would like to destroy was Sofia, she realised, feeling the first ice-cold frisson of fear.

Only fools don't feel fear, her brothers had told her, and Dom's small black eyes had turned as hard as marble. This was the other side of the smooth courtier's coin. It showed a man eaten up by jealousy for a prince who was twice the man he was, and for his Queen, who was vulnerable and kind, and now, incredible though it might seem to her, Sofia. 'I know you did it,' she said calmly.

'Did what?' Dom demanded in a disdainful tone.

'You're the only person who could possibly know the details that appeared to back up those scurrilous comments in the article. You're the only person with access to Prince Cesar's diary. You know all the dates and the events he attends. I ran through everyone else it could possibly be in my head on my way to the airport, and realised that no one else knows as much about the Prince's diary as you.'

A look of triumph sprang onto Dom's face. 'Are you admitting the details are true?'

'I'm not admitting anything. I'm saying you embroidered the facts to suit you and your master, Howard Blake, and I'm accusing you of colluding with Blake to introduce a suitor for the Queen's hand into court when Her Majesty was at her lowest ebb. You, above everyone, knows everything about the royal family, and how best to hurt them.'

Dom stiffened. She'd made a lucky guess but, having shown her hand, she was now in danger. Her brothers were out riding, and there was no sign of the SUV Cesar used on the ranch. He must have gone out somewhere, and there was no doubt that Dom, like his master Howard Blake, would stop at nothing to complete his mission of destroying everyone she loved. And she was alone with him in a kitchen full of potential weapons.

Contrary to popular belief, men could multitask. On his way to the airport, speakers in his muscle car read out his texts. There was nothing from Sofia. While he was confirming that, he was calling up his security team on a second, secure line. The first thing he'd done on waking and finding Sofia gone had been to ask his team, comprised entirely of ex-Special Forces, to institute a full-scale search for Sofia to make sure she was safe. Whatever had pulled her out of bed that morning had to be serious. Sofia was a serious-minded woman.

When she wasn't wild and abandoned in his arms.

He got an update from his team leader and smiled faintly. Nothing about Sofia could surprise him. 'This has only just happened?' he confirmed as he slowed the car.

His next call was to the airport, where his jet was ready and waiting. 'I won't be needing it,' he told his people.

His last call was to check the facts. He was a meticulous man.

An impersonal voice on the other end of the line informed him that the aircraft due to take Sofia home to Spain would board in around an hour, though as yet there was no sign of a Señorita Acosta on the checked-in passenger list.

Burning rubber, he screeched into a tyre-flaying U-turn and headed back the way he'd come. The road was straight and empty. He was driving a car with a top speed of over two hundred miles an hour. It would be rude to ignore the vehicle's potential.

As fast as it was, he still had time to think. If Sofia did something unusual, there was a good reason behind it. She'd slept in his arms. That was unusual. How had that made her feel? It had made him feel too much, which in itself was unusual. She'd trusted him, and that had touched him. What grabbed at his heart now and twisted it in knots was that whoever had their claws into Sofia wasn't ready to let go. And that put her in danger.

Howard Blake was another matter. He'd been dealt with. Cesar was not just meticulous, once he'd made up his mind he moved fast. He couldn't wait to tell Sofia that a cast-iron, signed and sealed document from Cesar's lawyers had landed in his inbox a couple of hours ago. His legal team had been working through the night to draw up a contract that would secure the financial future of Sofia's retreat for as long as it existed, thanks to an unbreakable trust that had been set up by none other than Howard Blake. Under Cesar's instructions.

To make doubly sure Blake's teeth were pulled, Cesar had purchased his newspaper empire, so Sofia was free to paint and ride to her heart's content, as well as help as many of those who needed her arm around their shoulder as she could.

The journey home was exasperating as possibility and probability jostled for position in his mind. Had Sofia read the second newspaper article yet? Would she laugh or cry when she did? His brain refused to stop whirring. Was she having second thoughts about sleeping with him? Not that much sleep had been involved. Was that why she'd left his bed? If she'd never reached the airport, but had returned to the *estancia* because she had guessed, as he had, that the trouble lay right there, then she could be in danger. Concern hit him like a punch in the gut. He put his car to the test. Two hundred miles an hour was not only achievable, but vital in this situation.

The black beast didn't let him down. The car did all but take flight.

'What are you going to do about this discovery of yours?' Dom sneered at Sofia as they faced each other in the kitchen. 'Do you plan to tell Cesar? Do you really think he'll believe you, after this second article? He might pretend not to believe you wrote it, but does he really know? Won't he doubt your honesty?'

With each question asked Dom moved a step closer. Sofia was backing up. They had almost reached the door. She planned to take her chances and escape as soon as she reached it. 'Of course I read the article on my phone,' she confirmed—anything to keep him talking. 'It was full of accusations, and insinuations about events supposedly taking place at the training camp.'

The lies had churned her stomach. With

Sofia's by-line at the top of the piece, it had made her relationship with Cesar read like a sting, calculated to trap him and prove him unworthy of the throne. If he believed those lies Cesar would cut her out of his life with surgical precision. Her brothers would never speak to her again. Funding would dry up for her retreat. It would have to close, leaving those she cared for with nowhere to go. She'd be a pariah, but that was nothing compared to the effect the damning article could have on a man who was brave and strong and principled, and who led by example, a prince who would one day be King. 'Where is Cesar?' she queried, heart clenching with lurid possibility. 'What have you done with him?'

'Me?' Dom touched his crisp, tailor-made shirt just short of where his heart should be. And then he lunged for her.

Dom's hand around her neck was removed so fast Sofia had no idea what had happened. One minute she was fighting a murderous opponent, and the next Dom was flat out on the kitchen floor with Cesar looming over him.

'Cesar!' It felt as if she'd shrieked his name but it sounded like a croak. He was at her side in an instant with his arm around her shoulders, bringing her so close in a clasp of relief that she could hardly breathe. 'Help—'

He released her in an instant and, holding her at arm's length, he stared down with relief, as well as something warmer and deeper. 'The conventional phrase, I believe, is, "Thank you".'

'When have we ever been conventional?' she managed hoarsely as she clutched her throat and coughed. 'But thank you.'

'Stop thanking me,' Cesar commanded in the softest whisper she'd ever heard. 'You landed a good blow there, making things easy for me, or why was that monster grabbing his crotch with one hand while attempting to strangle you with the other? If he'd had both his hands free—'

'But he didn't,' she soothed. 'And, anyway, you laid him out.' She'd checked.

'I've always been a bit of a scrapper,' she admitted. 'Four brothers?'

'I should have been here.' Cesar was in no mood for humour. Summoning his security team, he told them to remove the prisoner and lock him up.

'You got here as soon as you could,' Sofia argued. 'You came looking for me. That's all that matters.'

'I had to,' Cesar reflected grimly. 'I know you well enough to be confident you wouldn't leave the house without good reason. When I worked out what that reason could be, I knew I had to find you fast or you'd take things into your own hands. Are you sure you're okay?'

The look in his eyes touched her somewhere deep. 'I'm fine.' She stood back as two military types dressed in black entered the room.

'We have a lot to talk about,' he said.

'You read the article.' She knew he must have and felt a flutter of alarm.

'Of course,' Cesar confirmed.

'How did you know to find me here?'

'How do we know anything?' He frowned. 'Intuition? The assembly of known facts into a recognisable picture?'

Now the initial shock was over, her knees had turned to jelly. Cesar's steadying hand beneath her arm was more than welcome. It was one thing to be at the peak of physical fitness, and another to be attacked by someone who meant her harm, Sofia had discovered. She might have accepted that Dom was not the silky courtier he appeared, but his vicious lunge for her throat had really shocked her.

They went into Cesar's library. It was a cosy, reassuring room, with wood-panelled walls and comfortable seating.

'Take a seat on the sofa,' he invited. Crossing the room to a well-stocked bar, he poured a generous slug of fine brandy into a crystal glass. 'Here. Drink this...'

'I don't—'

'You do,' he insisted. 'And then we'll talk.'

She sipped and put the glass down, only then realising that the newspaper with its damning article—the same article that someone had *kindly* sent to her to make sure she didn't miss it—was lying open on the low table between them.

Closing her eyes, she exhaled shakily. 'How can I ever—'

'Don't.' Cesar raised his hand, palm flat. 'Let's get one thing straight. This is not your writing, not your fault, and nothing to do with you.'

'Without me, the campaign to discredit you wouldn't have got started,' she argued. Picking up the newspaper, she scanned the article she'd already read as if hoping it would somehow change into something she could read without feeling sick to the stomach that anyone could write such trash.

Cesar shrugged off her comment. 'Blake would have found someone else to do his dirty work.'

Breath shuddered out of her. She didn't want to be let off the hook so easily. 'The article appears under my name and will seem totally plausible to anyone who reads it. My brothers will read it and they can only think I'm betraying you again.'

'Then I'll set them straight, though I believe you're worrying unnecessarily. Do you really think they don't know what's been going on between us?'

What is going on between us? she wondered in the few seconds it took for Cesar to supply an answer to his own question but not to hers. 'I've known your brothers a long time—too long for them not to have picked up the vibes between me and their only sister. They're probably laughing their heads off right now as they read this garbage over the breakfast table.'

'Thanks. I'd rather not think about that, not when this could be so serious for you.'

'Believe me, I'm not taking it lightly,' Cesar assured her.

'And then there's your mother and sister. What will they think? This is so unfair, especially when it's clearly untrue.'

Maybe she had expected Cesar to argue this point, and say that there was something between them and that it was so deep that it transcended cheap gossip, but he remained silent, while she couldn't seem to stop words pouring from her mouth.

'All this rubbish about secret liaisons between us, and the things we do—' Her cheeks blazed red. 'With my by-line at the top of the article, it makes it seem I set you up.'

'But we know you didn't.'

'Of course I didn't, but this article is dangerous for you. You can't take it lightly.'

'I haven't,' Cesar assured her.

His eyes were cool and calculating. She knew instinctively that he would be reviewing plans he'd already made. Why didn't he share those plans with her? This cut right to the heart of why she wanted more from their relationship.

Her pulse jagged as Cesar shifted position, but it was only to ease his massive shoulders in a careless shrug. 'So everyone knows,' he observed, lips pressing down. 'What of it? Does it embarrass you to be linked to a prince? Or would you rather not be linked to me?'

'That's not it at all,' she protested, shaking her head with frustration.

'Then how about this?' He pinned her with his black stare. 'What if that prince asked you to marry him? Would you be mortified? Or relieved?'

'Relieved?' she asked incredulously. In her fantasies perhaps! 'I'd be horrified.'

Cesar's eyes narrowed. 'Should I be insulted?'

He didn't look insulted. Hand pressed to his chest, and with his black eyes scorching her face into an even hotter shade of red, Cesar appeared to be amused.

'I take it you're joking?' she said on a dry throat.

'Am I?'

Cesar managed to imbue those two words with so much heat and promise her body went wild. Her mind, however, was by now firmly back on track. 'If I were a drinker I'd ask for another brandy. I could never be princess material. You need someone—'

'What?' Cesar queried. 'Someone like me, do you mean, from a rarefied background raised on a diet of riches and privilege, while you were a raggedy tomboy, dragged up in a stable? It may surprise you to know I was an urchin, filthy and starving, plucked off the streets of Rome after being abandoned by my birth mother. I have a wonderful woman to call my mother, and to thank for hunting me down. The Queen saved me. It's as simple as that.'

Nothing about Cesar was ever simple, Sofia reflected, though she kept silent as he talked on. 'The Queen is the only real mother I've ever known. Her heart was big enough to make a home for the bastard son of her handmaid and the King, and she went on to bring me up as her own.'

For once Sofia was lost for words. Cesar

had never opened up about his past. However bad things got between them, the fact that he had chosen her to confide in meant a lot. 'I had no idea,' she said softly.

'About so many things,' Cesar confirmed, 'such as you can trust me with your life. Which brings me to repeat my question: Will you marry me?'

'I have to understand why you're asking me first,' she admitted.

'What is there to understand?'

'I understand why you bottle up your emotions, Cesar. To be abandoned at such a young age was bound to have repercussions—'

'I don't want to talk about me. I want to talk about you,' he insisted.

'By not talking about how you feel inside, you're letting the past win.'

'The past is the past. I've treated you badly.'

'And now I deserve a reward?' she asked, frowning.

'You're not one of my horses.'

'I'm glad you realise it.' A smile crept through.

'We're making progress?' he suggested.

'If you can express your feelings…'

'I do feel lots of things—especially when it comes to you. I feel lust, passion, frustration, tenderness...but most of all I feel an overwhelming certainty that I can't share my life with anyone but you. I love you, Sofia, with all my heart, my soul, and my body too. Marry me and let me keep you safe for ever.'

'You love me?' she whispered.

'How can you doubt it?'

Her head was spinning. She didn't have an answer right away. There was so much to take in that her heart felt as if it was in a vice. She'd barely recovered from the shock of Dom's attack, and then there had been the shame of seeing yet another newspaper article written in her name. Now she was faced with Cesar's bombshell proposal of marriage.

'I've said it before. I'm just not princess material, let alone queen.'

'Which is precisely why I think you'll be the most marvellous addition to the royal family,' Cesar insisted. 'You're what my people deserve—someone who will genuinely care for them and who's prepared to get their hands dirty. Not forgetting you'll have to put up with me.'

She searched Cesar's eyes for some hint of humour and found none. The past half an hour had brought about great change. Cesar had found her, saved her, and they'd confirmed the treachery of his aide. What was she waiting for? For the doubt demons to leave? Life was full of uncertainty. How you dealt with it was what mattered. The one thing you could not, must not do was to turn your back and walk away from the chance of happiness. 'Is this a serious proposal of marriage?'

'I would never joke about something so important,' Cesar promised with a steady look.

'But there's been no lead up, no hint of what you were thinking, no preparation—'

'For life?' he asked gently. 'How much preparation do you need? Seems to me you've been doing pretty well up to this point, and I believe this is the perfect solution to silence the critics following any fallout from the article. The Playboy Prince is ready to settle down—'

Just when she was ready to believe he could change and grow in the emotional sense, he slashed her belief into tiny pieces.'

'There's no point in dragging things out,' he said.

Life drained out of her but she was a fighter, which meant refusing to give up, especially when that meant giving up the man she loved. She wasn't going to let him go without a fight. 'What about tracing a possible path for our future first?' she asked crisply. 'What about describing your vision of the path we'll be walking down together. Or is this marriage just another business deal for you? Maybe it's a way for you to get your people onside. After all, everyone loves a royal wedding.'

Cesar looked shocked.

Grief, hurt and shame collided inside her. Receiving the proposal she'd dreamed of all her life in what amounted to bullet points was unbearable. She didn't need to be told that she wasn't a likely choice of bride for Prince Cesar of Ardente Sestieri, but to be made to feel that she was nothing more than a convenient solution for Cesar hurt like hell.

And then he made it worse.

CHAPTER FOURTEEN

'I AM A brutally honest man,' Cesar conceded with a grudging grin, 'but I'll admit that what I'm thinking doesn't come out the way I intend.'

'I get that, but it's what you're feeling too that needs expressing,' Sofia observed, 'and not just clinical thoughts when it comes to something as precious as marriage. What I don't want is for you to say something you don't mean.'

'But I do mean it,' he insisted with a hard stare. 'Every word.'

'With eyes as hard as flint?' she said, breaking up inside. 'Please, don't lie to me, Cesar. I don't understand how you can love me so much that you want to spend the rest of your life with me when I'll never be princess material.'

'That's the very reason I want to marry you. Haven't I told you that before?'

'Why can't you stop pretending that the marriage you propose is anything more than a convenient solution?'

'What do you want me to say, Sofia? I thought this was what you wanted.'

Tears sprang to her eyes. 'A marriage proposal that sounds more like a business deal?' she asked incredulously.

'Don't do this to me.' Cesar pulled back when she longed for him to move forward. 'I'm trying to be fair,' he insisted.

'So your future plans include a quirky horse-riding artist, said to have written defamatory articles about you? No smoke without fire,' she reminded him grimly. 'Does that sound like the perfect royal match to you? Will your countrymen go for it? Will the Queen stand and cheer when you tell Her Majesty our news?'

'Please, be calm,' Cesar insisted in a way that made her madder still. 'I've told you about my past so you know I'm not obvious prince material. Yet, here I am, not so very different from you. I wouldn't be asking you such a vital question if I thought you were a typical princess, spoiled, indulged, entitled, but none of those words describe you, Sofia.'

'No. I'm just the mug who fell in love with you,' she admitted, when she could finally draw an easy breath.

'You love me?'

'Of course I do!' she exclaimed heatedly.

'A fact that makes our marriage even more likely to succeed,' Cesar declared, without returning the compliment. 'So now we've got that sorted out, I'll give you a list of things to do in the lead up to our wedding.'

'No clipboard?' she asked heatedly. 'Don't tell me you forgot to bring it with you?'

Cesar appeared to be genuinely surprised. 'I'm sorry you think marriage to me such a dreadful prospect.'

Feelings erupted inside her. She wanted to go to him and hold him close, kiss him and drive the ghosts of the past away. Surely he could see that marriage between them was impossible. 'It's not a terrible prospect,' she protested. 'It's impractical. It wouldn't work. I've told you I love you—to which you showed no reaction at all. It's as if you don't value my love. '

'Nothing could be further from the truth,' he insisted. 'And I'd like to know what you base your conclusions on. I've made it plain from the outset that I'm not too grand for you. In fact, you come from a far more stable background. There must be another reason for your refusal. What is it, Sofia? What's holding you back?'

'I can't be with such an emotionless man. If this proposal of marriage is just a duty for you it wouldn't be honest of me to accept. I'd be selling your people short. We both would. They deserve more than a reluctant princess and a cold-hearted prince.'

'Cold-hearted?' Cesar queried frowning. 'Haven't I made it clear that you can have anything you want?'

'But I don't want material things. I want honesty, truth and love. Where are your feelings, Cesar? Where are you hiding them? Why can't you express them? Or do you think it's weak to show emotion?'

'Of course not.' He was growing heated now. 'I have deep feelings for my people, my family, and especially for you. What do you want me to say, Sofia? I know what I want. Marry me. Give me the chance to make you happy. You've nothing to fear from me. You're free to leave this marriage if you're unhappy, and of course that would be with a pension for life.'

That was the worst thing he could have said. Hope died inside her. It was as if her heart had shrunk until it resembled a walnut, shrivelled and dry.

'Haven't you listened to a word I've said?' she asked quietly. 'I don't want or need a pension for life. You make it sound as if I'm to be rewarded for deceiving your people.'

'I would never deceive my people,' Cesar protested, incredulous.

'With a grand royal wedding and a smiling bride?' she suggested. 'What would you call it? When I get married it will be for love, not for what I can get out of it. The era for business-like marriage mergers is long past!'

'But you'll be safe with me,' Cesar insisted, as if he couldn't believe what she'd said. 'I've bought up Howard Blake's empire so he'll never trouble you again. My former equerry Dom is currently in custody and will be judged by the highest court in the land. I intend to live my life protecting you and my people in every way I can. If you have even a gram of the renowned Acosta honour, surely you'll support me in this?'

'By marrying a man who cannot share his true feelings with me?'

It was tragic to think Cesar did have feelings, deep feelings, but he was incapable of expressing them in a way her heart could accept. In that, she supposed when she thought about it, they were both guilty.

'I'm sorry I've got no pretty words for you,' he said at last. 'That's just not who I am. Rest assured, I have no intention of forcing you to do anything you don't want to do. I'm relying on your good sense to get you through this.'

'You make it sound as if I must survive some unpleasant illness that can be dosed with a spoonful of sugar. I want so much more out of marriage than that. Love dies if it's all one-sided, and I couldn't bear—'

'To be abandoned again?' he suggested gently.

She took a moment to refocus, as he added, 'Losing your parents has left a gaping wound, and it's important for you to know that I understand. It will take time to prove I can help you heal, but I need the chance to do that.'

A tsunami of emotion threatened to overwhelm her. She had no doubt now that Cesar was sincere. Marrying him was a dream that could so easily become reality. All she had to do was say yes. But she wanted the best for Cesar too. He was a king amongst men, strong and principled, sincere, and she'd never find anyone like him again. Her heart yearned for nothing more than to twin with his. She truly couldn't fault him. And, of course, she loved him with all her heart.

'Maybe I could have said things better,' he conceded in the silence, 'but I'm not an orator, and I didn't plan to win your heart with words. I can see now that I've rushed things, but once I see a goal I go for it. There's been no time to woo you as you deserve, but I'll try to make it up to you. Most importantly, I'll care for you and keep you safe. Anything you need for the wedding can be ordered online,' he added, frowning as he compiled his mental list. 'If you need people to help you to prepare, call them now and put them on standby. Transport will be arranged for everyone who attends the ceremony. Make that clear to anyone you invite—'

'Cesar!' Her shout stopped him in his tracks. 'There can be no wedding. Have you listened to me at all?'

'The ceremony can take place in one week's time on my private island of Isla Ardente,' he said, unwittingly supplying the answer to her question.

'You're making plans for an event I have no intention of attending,' she pointed out.

'But that's the neatest way,' he insisted. 'When we're married we'll draw even bigger crowds to the charity matches. You'll need a ring, of course,' the man she loved with all her heart added, frowning, 'So why don't you browse the internet and choose something you'd like?'

For a moment the plastic rings that came in Christmas crackers flashed into her head. They would be perfect for a sham wedding.

'Better still, leave it to me!' he exclaimed, 'I have contacts at all the top jewellers—'

'Of course you do!' she interrupted. Doubt crept into the mix as she imagined all the expensive trinkets Cesar must have purchased over the years.

'There's no real urgency for an engagement ring' he added thoughtfully, 'though I expect you'd like something to show off at some point—'

'Show off?' she burst out.

'Whatever you like,' Cesar countered, with a smile that proved he was oblivious to her mounting frustration. 'Though we'll concentrate on finding a wedding band for now. We can sort out more jewellery later—'

'Stop this,' she exploded. 'Is this what your proposal boils down to? A sparkly stone and a pair of handcuffs disguised as a wedding band? Believe me, I'm not that desperate to get married. I'd sooner wed a walrus and feast on sea cucumbers than marry a man who opens his wallet without opening his heart.'

'But you want me,' Cesar stated flatly.

'If you're asking whether I like having sex with you, why not say so? I do. You're an amazing lover. Would I like to have more sex with you? Yes, of course, but having sex is very different from planning to spend the rest of your life with someone.' It hurt to even think those words, let alone say them. Being intimate with Cesar had meant *everything* to her. She'd given herself completely, freely, trustingly and lovingly, but had it meant the same to him?

'Perhaps you see things differently,' he suggested.

'I see you clearly.' She drew on every bit of control she had to keep her voice steady and her eyes direct. 'The unexpressed feelings you have are possibilities waiting to happen. You get angry when you can't express yourself, but I don't need flowery words any more than I need expensive gifts. I just want you to be honest with me—with both of us.'

Cesar frowned. 'Are you frustrating my plans?'

'There you go again,' she said with a hint of desperation in her voice. 'We should be getting married because we want nothing more than to be together. Not because it suits your agenda. Open your heart, Cesar. Let me know how you truly feel.'

'But we could save a country together.'

'As well your reputation,' she observed shrewdly.

'Not to mention yours,' Cesar countered. 'Just tell me what you want. Name your price.'

'Name my price?' she repeated in a strangled whisper.

'Clumsy words,' he admitted, raking his hair with frustration. 'I told you I'm no good with words.'

But the damage had been done.

'This marriage will lift the mood of my people—'

'You can't even call it *our* marriage,' she burst out, unable to keep silent any longer.

'It would instantly make a mockery of the article,' Cesar continued as if she hadn't spoken. 'Despite what the writer suggests, there was no seedy liaison between us at the training camp but an unfolding love story that will now have a beautiful ending.'

'Is that what you truly believe?' she asked. Hope pushed its way through the tangle of weeds like a green shoot.

Only to be trampled on.

'I've told you to name your price, Sofia, so please tell me what you would like to make this marriage happen. Please, appreciate that this is a difficult situation for both of us and time is short.'

She shook her head sadly. 'Not for you. You seem to have it all worked out. Would you like my bank details for a money transfer or will you pay me in pieces of silver?'

'Stop it,' Cesar advised calmly. 'If you think about this logically, you'll come to agree that nothing could be more uplifting for my people than a wedding between us.'

How could they be so far apart? She hid an agony of disillusionment behind another question. 'Have you discussed this with my brothers?'

'I thought you were old enough to make your own decision.'

'As I thought you experienced enough in the ways of the world to know what's right,' she fired back. 'What you're proposing is a marriage of convenience—convenient for you, that is.'

'All I want is for you to be happy and safe.'

'You have a strange way of showing it.'

'Do I?' Cesar asked, seeming perplexed.

'Asking me to be your wife surely requires me to say yes before arrangements can be made? A little more thought and preparation generally goes into these things than the advice to "Browse the Internet".'

Cesar raked his hair. 'But you can have anything you want.'

'*Things* don't matter.' She waited, and then waited some more while Cesar stared at her as if she was speaking a foreign language. 'I give up,' she said at last. 'Seduction might be your forte, but when it comes to wooing a woman you have zero idea. It takes more than a vault full of priceless jewels to build trust, and more than pomp and ceremony to impress me. If you had suggested a small, informal barefoot wedding on the beach of your private island, with just a band of twine around my finger and some fresh flowers in my hair—'

'Done! That's an excellent idea.'

'What?' She stared at Cesar in horror.

'I'll get my team on it right away, and then I'll present my beautiful bride to our people at a formal blessing in the cathedral in the capital sometime later.'

'Best find yourself a bride first,' Sofia advised before she left the room.

* * *

Well, that went well. Cesar paced up and down, frowning, long after Sofia had slammed the door and disappeared. Her final words had been like a well-aimed blow to the chin, but instead of knocking him out they had knocked him into a different mind-set. He'd been so preoccupied, facing the threat to him and Sofia, that he had instinctively moved into leading and planning mode, which on this occasion had involved a wedding ceremony, when Sofia had needed proper reassurance that he loved her before, not after, a proposal of marriage.

He had assumed she would realise that his offer was heartfelt, but now he realised she'd thought it a ruse to distract his people from the latest gossip. The thought of marriage to Sofia had struck him like a bombshell, mainly because marrying anyone else was unthinkable. That nightmare was only exceeded by the thought of Sofia marrying someone else. He loved her with all his heart, he realised now, but had he left it too late?

Years back, when he'd been in the army and his comrades had been getting married one by one, he had envied them for the love they shared, and for the company they could look forward to with someone who loved them unreservedly. Marriage had once seemed an elusive possibility for the so-called Playboy Prince, but he had longed for nothing more than to settle down and build a family...if only he knew how.

Sofia had made that achievable. She was no spoiled, milksop princess, staring haughtily down her nose at his people while acting as everyone's friend. He wanted a real woman with real character, someone who would take him to task, and here she was, but had he messed up the best chance he'd ever have?

He had to find a way around this. He wanted Sofia to be his wife, not to smooth over the cracks of the article or because it made sense but because he adored her and he wanted her in every way there was. It was hard to express his feelings, but if he kept on trying, maybe he'd get better at it. He had to or he'd lose her for good. And there would never be another Sofia.

Time was short, and the task ahead of him was not just demanding, but would normally take months to complete. How long did it take to woo a woman? He had no idea. It had never been necessary in the past. He prided himself on being a meticulous organiser, but where this was concerned he was in the dark. How long would it take to convince Sofia she could trust him completely when he was starting his campaign from such a low base?

Happiest when he was doing something, he called a meeting for everyone to attend the following morning before training. Until then, guessing Sofia had had enough of his 'bulldozing ways', as she'd called them, he keep himself busy riding, working out, swimming, reading, sparring in the gym with her brothers—anything but risk speaking to Sofia before he was ready. He was good at planning and hopeless at wooing, but when it came to winning Sofia's heart, he was on a mission to succeed.

CHAPTER FIFTEEN

PUNISHING HER PILLOW for the lack of anything else to thump, she sobbed like a baby and railed against fate. How could a man who had risen like a phoenix from the ashes of his childhood, with a brain to rival Einstein's and personal success that exceeded most people's, be so dense as to imagine that a pretty ring and the promise of riches could find their way to her heart?

She didn't want that with Cesar. She wanted new paints, a puppy and a kitten, and a bridle for her horse. She wanted time together to laugh and be silly, and plan a future that didn't involve self-interest and what she had to gain. There was so much she wanted to do, and all she needed was the chance to get out there and do it. The idea of extending her retreat to encompass an entire country, where no one felt left out or forgotten, would be a dream come true. And, yes, she was a bit of a dreamer, but wouldn't Cesar be the perfect counterbalance to that?

She was glad when the phone rang. Maybe that would shake her out of this noisy, messy pity party. 'Hello?'

'Sofia?'

Her heart stopped beating.

'Cesar here.'

As if she didn't know, as if her entire body, mind and soul hadn't recognised that deep, husky voice the moment he'd spoken. A quick analysis of his tone said this was an exploratory call to judge her mood, as she was attempting to judge his.

'Are you all right? Sofia? Say something.'

'I'm fine.' She sniffed. 'A bit of a cold coming on, that's all.'

'Good. I've called a meeting tomorrow morning before training to give the official line on the latest article. I trust you will attend?'

She was confused and not a little angry. '*Your* official line?'

'Yes.'

'Don't I have a say in this?'

'I'll speak first, and then open the floor to questions.'

'Cesar...' She hesitated, frowning. 'Do you ever listen to yourself?'

'You mean playback when I've been interviewed? Sometimes—'

'No. I mean right now,' she informed him. 'If you could only come down from Planet Exalted and speak to me as an equal.'

'I do,' he protested.

'Good, because I'd like to stand at your side and give my own version of events, if that's okay with you?'

There was heavy silence for a good few moments and then he said stiffly. 'If that would make you happy.'

'It would.'

Perhaps she should be angry with Cesar but she had grown up with four brilliant brothers—brilliant in the sense of their keen, ever-seeking minds, and brilliant because they were so good to her—but they often saw no further than their noses, especially where matters of the heart were involved. 'What time tomorrow?'

Cesar gave a time. She thanked him and

promised to be there. Putting the phone down, she went to stare at her reflection in the mirror. Very nice if red eyes and runny noses were your thing. Not such a good look for a woman who was about to buckle on her armour to fight for the heart of a man she couldn't bring herself to let go. Never mind what Cesar could do for her. What could she do for him?

He felt like a child on Christmas Day waking early to check that everything was as it should be when the moment came when gifts could be opened in a shower of discarded paper and laughter. A run, a ride, a workout in the gym, and a swim before his shower, and he was ready for what would be a very different day.

Dressed in riding gear, he greeted Sofia's brothers in the arena. Sofia was already there, with his favourite mutt Bran at her heels. He took it as a sign. The hound viewed him with his big, intelligent brown eyes, assessing his mood as Cesar was assessing Sofia's.

'Good boy, Bran,' he soothed as the dog trotted over to him. He dug out some treats.

'Well?' Sofia's youngest and wildest brother Xander demanded, snapping a whip impatiently against his boots. 'You called this meeting. What do the two of you want to talk about? We've got training to do.'

'Cesar has asked me to marry him.'

Sofia's voice carried clear and strong in the vaulted space. A good few seconds of deafening silence passed before Sofia's older brother Raffa commented, 'He must have enjoyed your article.'

'I can do without your sarcasm, Raffa,' she scolded.

Her brother shrugged.

The only four men in the world who could possibly, in a concerted effort, take Cesar down were staring at him as if his remaining time on earth would be short. That didn't bother him. What did concern him was Sofia's blood-drained face. She was standing in front of them at her most vulnerable. He lost no time reassuring her.

'I'm here to ask you, Sofia's brothers, to do me the honour of allowing me to ask for your sister's hand in marriage.' Pretty words could trip off his tongue when he was desperate. 'I want to do everything properly,' he explained with a long look at Sofia. 'And in case you're wondering, I've already asked Sofia to marry me and she said no. My timing was out, but I'll make that right.'

'If Sofia said no, that's an end of it,' Xander insisted, slashing a whip impatiently against his booted calf.

'No.' Sofia held up her hand as she stepped forward. 'At least do Cesar the courtesy of listening to him—as I shall.'

'So talk,' Xander growled.

'Have you engineered this proposal to spare you the accusations in the latest article?' Raffa demanded suspiciously.

'Of course not.' He could state that with a clear conscience. 'If there had never been an article, I would want to marry Sofia. For me, there's no one like her. No one remotely close. And I love her.' He had to hope he wasn't too late. 'Humble pie is not a dish I eat with any frequency,' he admitted with a self-deprecating shrug, 'but this is different, this is for Sofia, and I'll grovel if that's what it takes.'

'My sister has brought you to your knees?' Dante suggested, failing to hide his amusement.

'She did,' he confirmed. 'I've promised myself to listen and act in future, rather than the other way around. I think we all know that your sister had nothing to do with those articles. My equerry, Domenico, is the culprit, and has been dealt with, while his master Howard Blake will be funding Sofia's retreat, as well as any future retreats she cares to open, out of his substantial bank account.'

'How on earth did you get him to agree to that?' Xander remarked with a glance at his brothers.

'I bought his company with a binding agreement that ensures Blake signs away part of those funds to Sofia's retreats each year. So now all that remains is your answer...'

'Sofia?' Dante asked.

Not realising what he had arranged with Blake, Sofia appeared shocked numb, and could only nod her head briefly. 'You did this for me?' she managed finally.

'Useless with words, better with actions,' he confirmed with a smile.

'I can't believe what you've done!' she exclaimed.

'But it pleases you?' he confirmed.

'Securing the future of my work? Of course. I can't thank you enough.'

'Okay, you two,' Dante interrupted, holding up his hand as he prepared to mount his pony. 'Let's call a halt to this. We've got training to do. As I understand it, Cesar is asking our permission to court Sofia with the intention of making an honest woman of her—a princess, in fact. We can hardly deny him that opportunity.'

Sofia's brothers agreed with a knowing laugh. When they finally quietened down, Xander said, 'Have you ever asked permission to do anything in your life, Cesar?'

'Never,' he admitted bluntly. 'But this is different. This is Sofia.' And these were men of honour that he was proud to call friends.

'Are you sure you know what you're taking on?' Raffa asked with amusement.

'I've got some idea, but I'll take her in spite of her faults.' This ended in a chorus of good-natured catcalls, and then he added, 'Because I love her with all my heart.'

'Should we start the training now?' Sofia suggested, a warm note in her voice as she winked at Jess and gave him a lingering smile.

Suitor-in-training would be an accurate description for him. How good it felt. Triumph surged through him as he sprang into the saddle and wheeled his hot-wired pony around.

By the end of that day's training Sofia was mentally and physically exhausted. It had been almost impossible to keep her mind on training after Cesar's impassioned declaration. She kept glancing at him as if to make sure this new, improved Cesar wasn't a figment of her imagination. Nope. He seemed pretty real to her. Her brothers said nothing more about it, and it was a thrill to feel much of their camaraderie returning. Cesar saying she was innocent was enough to convince them. She couldn't thank him enough for that. She'd take brotherly love any day over a flashy diamond ring.

When the session ended, Cesar dismounted first. Handing his reins to a groom, he insisted on helping her down. 'You've worked so hard your legs will buckle under you.'

'My legs will obey my commands,' she insisted, stubbornly as usual.

Wrong. Her legs did not obey. They buckled. Cesar's hand steadied her, but he made no move to crowd her or do any more than set her firmly on her feet.

'See you at supper,' he said.

So much for romance, she reflected wryly, wondering how and when Cesar's idea of wooing would actually show itself.

Before cleaning up for the evening ahead, she went to check on the ponies. Bran trotted along at her heels. She stopped at one of the stalls where a pony belonging to Cesar was receiving attention. Glad of something to take her mind off Cesar, she sent the groom away to enjoy her supper and set about applying the poultice herself. Soft words and the cooling relief soon had the pony's ears pricked again.

'Problem?'

'Cesar!' She wheeled around at the sound of his voice. 'No. She'll be fine for the match if you rest her tomorrow.'

'I guess we're all feeling the strain of Jess's training,' he observed.

Sofia was feeling the strain of something. She smiled faintly. Cesar didn't appear to be any the worse for wear as he rested back against the wall of the stall. In fact, he had never looked more startlingly dynamic, with his deep tan, close-fitting breeches and plain dark polo shirt. His thick black hair was all messed up and catching on his stubble, while his eyes, his lips—everything about him... He was so hot it felt like being hit by an electric charge. She dropped her gaze, only for it to land on well-worn leather riding boots hugging hard-muscled calves. Swallowing deeply, she looked away to concentrate on the pony. 'See you in the ranch house when I've finished here—'

'Change of plan,' he announced, pulling away from the wall. 'I'm cooking tonight.'

'You're...?'

'You can close your mouth now,' he said, his lips curving in a grin. 'My mother the Queen taught me some campfire specials.'

'That seems unlikely.'

'My mother is a very surprising woman.'

'I don't doubt it.' There was something shining in Cesar's eyes—a warmth she hadn't seen before, and affection. And was that hope that she'd agree to his suggestion? A camp-fire supper was a small thing, but it marked a big step forward in their relationship. She wanted nothing more than to be close to him, normal with him, and what better way than singeing sausages over a campfire? Did she really mean that much to him? He couldn't have been more forthright when he spoke to her brothers,

'See you around eight o'clock—lower field,' he instructed.

She smiled inwardly at his tone of voice. Some things never changed.

Give him a chance, her inner voice insisted.

'Lower field?' she queried. That was one she hadn't heard of.

'Anyone will tell you where to find me. Don't be late.'

'I won't,' she promised softly.

Sofia rode out to meet him, by which time he'd lit a fire and their meal was cooking, though the most important ingredient had just arrived.

'*Cesar!*' she exclaimed as she dismounted. 'What have you done?'

'Brought an easel and paints along to join us. I thought you might be missing your painting, and there's nothing more beautiful than sunset at the river. I thought you could sketch an outline, and maybe finish the painting before you leave for Isla Ardente. That way you can hang the painting anywhere you choose—here, or in my house on the island.'

'You mean you'd seriously hang my painting in your ranch house?'

His lips pressed down as he pretended to consider this. 'If it's any good.' And when she cuffed him, he added, 'It could be your ranch house if you agree to become my wife.' She stared at the easel and paints, and then at him. 'Do I get a second chance to make this right?'

'Nothing could make me happier...' she breathed, eyes wide, lips parted seductively '...than a reunion with my easel and paints.'

A laugh cracked out of him. '*Touché!*'

'But seriously,' she added, 'this really does make me happy. Thank you.'

She looked beautiful. Her hair was loose, wild and tangled after her ride, and her cheeks were flushed pink. She'd dressed for a picnic in casual clothes—a cotton shirt in a faded check print tucked into a pair of clean jeans.

'You didn't need to do all this. You still don't,' she said. 'Putting things back to normal with my brothers is more than enough for me. I can never thank you enough for all you've done.'

'I don't want your thanks any more than you want lavish gifts. All I want is your hand in marriage, for no better reason than I love you.'

'Nicely put,' she teased, but the smile on her face was one of pure happiness. And then she dropped a bombshell. 'Though we don't have to get married. You do know that, don't you?'

His gut clenched. 'What do you mean?'

'Just that you silenced the gossips when you exposed Howard Blake and his accomplice Dom. Your country applauds you, your mother has never doubted you, and I... I only want you to be happy.'

'Without you?' He frowned. *No. No. No.* This was supposed to be perfect. An evening together in a glorious setting, away from all distractions was their chance to put the past behind them, to discard it like an old notebook crammed full of notes that were meaningless now so they could start again on a clean sheet.

'We do have to get married,' he argued quietly, feeling as if his entire existence depended on his next few words. 'I can't live without you. I don't want to try.'

'You mean it, don't you?' she asked him softly.

'Every word,' he stated firmly. 'If you can see this as base camp, we'll start our journey here. I can't promise there won't be difficulties along the way but we'll get through them. Are you up for starting tonight? See where it takes us?'

Sofia didn't speak for the longest few seconds of his life, during which the road ahead of him loomed bleakly at the prospect that she might say no.

'I'd be honoured to accept your proposal,

on the understanding that this is a true partnership.'

'Of equals,' he confirmed.

'In that case...'

'Kiss me?' he suggested.

'What's keeping you?'

The meal was singed to a cinder by the time he had answered that question. Fortunately, his chefs had left him well prepared, and Sofia declared the remaining food some of the best she had ever tasted.

'And you prepared all this yourself?' she exclaimed with approval.

He would start as he intended to continue—with the truth. 'I put my name to it,' he admitted, staring up through half-closed eyes. 'I also warmed it up, which took a certain degree of skill.'

'Save your skill for the bedroom,' Sofia scolded.

He would, but restraint was killing him.

'Please thank your chefs from me, and tell them the food was delicious.'

'Don't I get any credit?'

'For that? Or for this?'

When Sofia kissed him, he congratulated

himself on not following the impulse to thoroughly ravish her. True to his vow, he'd store up that desire and would suffer a straining groin for as long as it took. But not for too long, he trusted.

A welcome distraction came when Sofia went to examine her easel and paints. Even in jeans she looked like a queen, he reflected as she walked to the riverbank. His groin tightened on cue, reminding him that where Sofia was concerned there was no such thing as too much sex. To ramp up the agony, he'd chosen a setting that was perfect for lazy lovemaking. The grass was lush and deep, and it would be soft and fragrant beneath then. The night breeze would cool them— *Dio!* He wanted her. Now he knew the true meaning of agony.

'Are these artists' materials really mine?' she asked, turning to greet him as he joined her at the easel.

'They're all yours',' he confirmed, thinking how beautiful she looked with the last rays of the sun bathing her in a cloud of light. Looping his hands loosely around her waist, he encouraged, 'Go to it. I can't wait to see what you come up with.'

'I know what you've come up with,' she scolded. 'And this is only our first date.'

'But I can kiss you,' he said, starting by kissing her neck.

'You can,' she agreed. Her voice trembled with a throb of excitement so her next words were unexpected. 'But that's all you can do,' she insisted.

Unseen, he ground his teeth until he was sure they would shatter.

They cantered back together. Wind in her hair and Cesar at her side, she had never been happier. Her lips were bruised from his kisses, though the frustration of holding back from progressing those kisses was pure torture. And now the idea of marrying a prince, and therefore becoming a princess, was niggling at her. Cesar's life was so very different from hers. No way was she regal material. Born a tomboy, she was happiest and most relaxed at an easel or in the saddle. Cesar was rich and she was poor, having invested every penny of her inheritance in the retreat.

'You're very quiet,' he commented as they slowed their horses on the approach to the yard.

'Happily contented,' she said as she dismounted. That wasn't strictly true. She wanted Cesar's arms around her and his naked body, warm and demanding, against hers.

Springing down from the saddle, he led their horses to the stable. 'I'll see them settled down and then I'm going to bed. I suggest you do the same. Remember, we've got training in the morning.'

She didn't want to sleep alone, and had expected Cesar to change his mind about wooing her 'properly', she realised now. 'I hadn't forgotten, but thank you,' she called to him on a dry throat.

With one last, brief sideways glance Cesar raised an amused brow and walked away.

CHAPTER SIXTEEN

THIS WAS KILLING HIM. Taking things slowly did not suit him. Cesar ground his teeth as he led their horses back into the stable complex. Having not only read the menu but having tasted it, holding back where Sofia was concerned was up there with the hardest things he'd ever had to do. Hard being a word he wanted to expunge from his mind right now.

Taking things slowly was the sensible thing to do, he persuaded himself as he removed his horse's tack. In Sofia's case, it was the only way. But that didn't mean he had to like it or that it was going to be easy. He had never held back, whether in the army, business, polo or anything else, but having promised to court Sofia as she deserved—when what he wanted was to throw her over his shoulder, carry her off to bed and make love to her until her legs refused to hold her up—he would stick to the original plan. But if there was one thing this experience had taught him it was that celibacy was massively overrated.

She couldn't sleep that night. Things were so bad she had actually left her bedroom door open a crack in the hope that Cesar might find his way in. No such luck. Thin strands of lilac light were already pushing their way through the curtains. Everyone would be up soon, and there was no sign of him. Not even a text.

Scrambling out of bed, she took a quick shower and got dressed, ready for the morning training session. Leaving her room, she crept down the corridor. Everyone was still asleep. Her next stop was the ranch house. Running across the yard, she entered the main house through the back door with the key they'd all been given in case they felt hungry when the cookhouse was closed. Setting to, she made pancakes, something she was rather good at, if she did say so herself. Loading a tray with coffee and freshly squeezed juice, she loaded it with pancakes for two and went to say a proper thank you to Cesar.

Backing into his bedroom, she put the tray

down on the nightstand by his bedside. His pillows looked as if they'd been punched into oblivion and his covers were in a knot. There was no sign of Cesar but she could hear the shower running. Her throat dried with anticipation. Would he stride out of the bathroom naked, fully clothed, or would he have a towel looped around his waist?

'Sofia!'

Naked.

Okay.

Securing her wide-eyed gaze to his, as if to prevent that gaze from straying, he reached for a robe, handily tossed onto a nearby chair, and shrugged it on.

Too late. Her gaze had already strayed. Her breath quickened and her lips parted. 'Pancakes?'

'I could do with something to eat,' Cesar confirmed, though she thought she detected a wicked smile on his wicked mouth. And was his robe left unfastened on purpose?

'You'll catch cold.'

'Not a chance,' he said, padding purposefully in her direction. Rather than reaching for the food she had prepared, or pouring a cup of coffee, he reached for her. Cupping her face in his hands, he whispered, 'You look so beautiful this morning. And what a thoughtful thing to do.'

She could have drowned in those eyes. She still might.

Bringing her close, Cesar kissed her good morning.

His kisses were like incendiary devices to her senses. Closing her eyes, she dragged deep on the heady mix of soap and warm, clean man. If she could have this for the rest of her life, she would be the happiest woman on the face of the earth.

'Coffee?'

She realised Cesar was speaking to her. 'I made the breakfast for you,' she insisted. 'It's nothing much, just another thank-you for the easel and paints, and the delicious picnic last night.'

'I have a confession to make.'

'You do?' Apprehension gripped her. She should have known this was too good to be true.

'If we're going to make this work, we have to be honest with each other. Correct?'

'Correct,' she agreed tensely.

Cesar's burning gaze lit with humour. 'I want you, and it isn't in my nature to wait.'

Laughter drove her tension away, and then their fingers brushed as she accepted the cup of coffee he'd poured. How was it she'd never noticed before how seductive the brush of a hand could be? 'Pancakes first?' she suggested.

Cesar laughed. 'Seriously?'

'Of course seriously,' she insisted, trembling with excitement inside. 'Do they look that bad?'

'They look absolutely delicious. Do your worst,' he encouraged.

Oh. She forced herself to brighten. 'Sugar?' she asked with a smile.

Cesar's answer was to yank her close enough to drown in his eyes. 'We're going to be very late for training,' he promised. But then he gently disentangled himself and started eating pancakes.

The result was a frustrating day. Sex helped to wipe her mind clear of doubt, Sofia realised, reeling with exhaustion by the time training ended. Doubt had been her constant companion since losing her parents, and it was back full force now. What if Cesar's proposal was only to prove to her brothers that his intentions were honourable? Once they left this training camp hothouse behind, and life returned to normal, would Cesar come to realise that he didn't love her after all?

The temptation to confront him with these concerns battled with her desire to squeeze every last drop of happiness out of their time together. Remembering how Cesar had touched her face so tenderly last night didn't help, and only made her realise how much she'd miss him if Cesar came his senses and realised that marrying her would be wrong. Tears stung her eyes as she walked back to the stable. Thank goodness Jess had pushed them hard. She'd had less time to think. But now—

'Hey, you!'

Cesar's call stopped Sofia in her tracks halfway across the stable yard. He was tossing a bucket of ice-cold water from the well over his impossibly magnificent half-naked self. She closed her eyes to that, and to him, or she tried to.

'Where are you rushing off to?' he asked with a frown, staring at the large, zip-up bag she was carrying. It contained all her loose possessions from the tack room. She was on her way to add it to the stack of luggage in her room.

'Hey, yourself.' Her face burned with guilt at having been caught out. She should have told Cesar before arranging her journey home, but once she'd realised the best thing to do was to give them both space, she had rushed through the arrangements, knowing that if she stopped to think too much about it, she'd never go through with her plan. She'd confided in Jess and had promised she'd be back in time for the match. Jess clearly didn't agree with what she was doing but had enough sense to keep those thoughts to herself, confining herself to comments on Sofia's fitness, saying that if she kept up her training back home in Spain, Sofia would be more than ready for the match.

'I couldn't get an internet connection in my room,' she told Cesar now, 'so I'm off to the cookhouse to see if I can sort out something there.' She was a terrible liar, and he knew it.

'Internet?' he probed. 'Why don't you use mine at the ranch house?'

'I never thought of that.'

'Really?' He quirked a disbelieving brow.

If she stayed another hour her heart would shatter. However Cesar dressed it up, a marriage of convenience would never work between them. Her heart would break before their union had a chance.

You seem preoccupied, Sofia.'

'No.' She shook her head.

'Wistful, then.'

'Memories can do that,' she admitted.

'Live in the moment and be happy.' Cesar spread his arms wide as if to welcome her into his world. 'Don't look so worried. What you see is what you get.'

Which was not just a prince, she thought as he stared down. Cesar was a deeply principled man who wielded great power and wealth. His destiny was preordained. She'd been lucky enough to cross his path briefly, but that was all. There could never be anything more between them. She had to help

Cesar to see that he must forget the idea of marrying her, and if that meant leaving him so that in time he forgot her, then that was what she would do.

Love involved sacrifice sometimes, and this was one of those times. The threat of scandal was already fading, its roots stamped out. The press had new headlines. The people of Ardente Sestieri were confident in their prince. It was just Sofia who was out of step. But the one thing she owed him above everything else was honesty. 'Is there somewhere we can talk?'

'No,' he grated out, surprising her with the harshness in his tone. 'There is not. And you're not leaving me,' he stated firmly. 'I won't let those demons from the past destroy you. You have to be brave to love completely, and I know you can.'

'Cesar—please... You don't understand. I can't do this to you. I have to leave. It's for the best.'

'Whose best? Yours?'

She lifted the bag. He took it from her. She wrestled it back. 'I'm going home. You can't stop me. I should have told you before, but—'

'There wasn't time?' he suggested. 'Forgive me, Sofia, but where is your loyalty now?'

'I won't let the team down. I'll be back for the match. We both need time to cool down and think, and then you'll see that I'm right.'

'Oh, will I?' Cesar challenged fiercely. 'When are you going to stop running, Sofia? You can't escape your parents' death, no matter how far or how fast you run.'

'What?' The bag dropped from her hands. 'Is that what you think this is about?'

'I don't think, I know it is,' Cesar assured her. 'How do I know? Because my emotions have been strangled for years. I resented you to begin with for the way I saw myself reflected in the way that you behave—the self-inflicted isolation, the determination to help others at whatever cost to yourself, the overwhelming urge to win, to race, to exhaust yourself—and it still doesn't blot out the pain.

'It doesn't work, Sofia! Because when you've finally run yourself into the ground and lie down on your bed at night the pain's still there. And it will be with you until you deal with it.'

Sofia seemed to visibly shrink in front of

him. 'How do you do that?' she asked him in a small voice.

'You learn coping strategies. You remember the good times as well as the bad. I'm still a work in progress,' he admitted. 'But we can fix this together. I won't lose you now.'

'You can't stop me leaving.'

'True.' Sofia was ready to be hurt some more, he realised as her dark eyes searched his. 'I would never stop you with force,' he assured her, his voice full of understanding. 'You have to decide you want to stay, just as you have to move forward instead of constantly looking back. You can do it,' he said gently, 'because now you're not on your own, you have me.'

She exhaled on a faint smile. 'How do you know all this?'

'Because I still have pain here.' He pressed a hand against his heart. 'I just hide it better than you.'

Taking hold of Sofia's shoulders in a loving grip, he brought her to face him. 'I know how you feel because I've spent most of my life hiding my feelings. When my father was killed, when I lost comrades in the forces, and when my mother took up with a man who only ever meant her harm and I felt I'd lost her too, I hurt like hell, but I've become an expert over the years when it comes to hiding my true thoughts.' He frowned. 'I can't do that with you, Sofia. Stay with me, and I promise I'll make you happy, and we'll work through this together.'

She wanted to stay with Cesar more than anything, but if she agreed to marry him, what would happen when the training camp ended and the matches were over, and she was no longer outstanding in any way? She'd be plain Sofia Acosta again—a great rider, with some small skill in painting pictures and a retreat to run. She wasn't suited to royal life.

Cesar needed someone with style and panache, who could sit beside him, exuding elegance and grace, and who would behave properly at all times. Not some country bumpkin with grime under her nails and dog hair and slobber on her clothes. 'I'm just not suitable.'

'For what?'

Cesar's eyes had a wicked glint, and his

mouth was tugging up at one corner in the way she loved. 'Don't do this,' she warned.

'Do what?'

'Seduce me with a look. Make me change my mind—' She broke off, seeing her brothers with Olivia and Jess crossing the yard. Let off the hook, she yelled, 'Hello!'

'Come on, Sofia,' Cesar insisted, reclaiming her attention. 'You're only allowed so much time to bury your head in the sand and pretend this isn't the best thing that has ever happened to either of us.'

Come on, Sofia, her inner voice echoed. *Prince or not, Cesar is the best thing that ever happened to you.*

'Dump that bag in the barn,' he suggested. 'Join everyone in the cookhouse. You must be hungry after training.'

Was she giving Cesar another chance or herself? Sofia wondered as they headed off to the cookhouse together.

For the first time he could remember, no one teased them when he and Sofia finally sat down in the cookhouse to eat their meal.

'Okay?' He took hold of her hand in full

sight of everyone present and brought it to his lips. There was a moment of complete still-ness, but no one commented, and after a moment or two the buzz of conversation started up again. He wouldn't have cared whether or not they were accepted as a couple, but it felt good to have the acknowledgement of those closest to them that he was taking his wooing plans forward.

'Getting there,' Sofia whispered back with an intimate smile. 'You've given me something to think about,' she admitted. 'A lot to think about, in fact.'

'Like another date night?' he suggested.

'Only if it comes with pizza and a bottle of beer.'

'I can sort that,' he confirmed. 'Whatever your heart desires.'

'My heart isn't as sophisticated as yours'—'

'No doubts,' he interrupted. 'We're in this together, remember?'

She thought about this for all of two seconds before adding chocolate ice cream to her list of requirements for their second date.

'Deal.' He held out his hand across the table to shake hers. And never wanted to let go.

Now they got catcalls. 'Find a room,' one of Sofia's brothers bellowed.

They shut him out. The amused glance they shared said it all. Sofia couldn't have been happier to be teased by her brothers. When'd she first arrived at the training camp the relationship between Sofia and her brothers had been strained, to put it mildly, but now she was elated to find it back to normal. They should expect more of this, he accepted wryly as they rose as one from the table. Fingers linked, they walked out of the cookhouse without a backward glance.

CHAPTER SEVENTEEN

THE FACT THAT chocolate and pizza could taste so good on a dish called Sofia would bring a smile to his face for the rest of his life. Date night had started innocently enough with Sofia cutting pizza into slices while he wedged lime into bottles of beer. They talked, relaxed, laughed, and talked some more.

But the more they laughed, the more sexual tension soared between them. Fingers brushed, eyes met, gazes steadied, lingered, until something had to give. Drawing Sofia into his arms, he meshed his fingers through her hair and kissed her as tenderly as if this was the first time they'd touched.

'Why are you always so impatient?' he growled against her mouth when she moved her body seductively against his.

'Have you looked in a mirror recently?'

'So you only want me for my body?'

'We can start with that,' she teased. 'But actually,' she added, turning serious, 'I want all of you, every bit of you, even the bits you didn't know you had. I want to hold your secrets in my heart and laugh with you as we've laughed tonight. I want to grow old with you.'

'You don't want to know all my secrets,' he assured her.

'Yes, I do,' she argued in a whisper, 'but you'll tell me in your own time. There are things you don't know about me, and a lot I don't know about you, but we can find out together. And sorry to ask but do you think we could stop talking now?'

'You are a shameless hussy.'

'Thank goodness you made me that way.'

'As you're naked in my kitchen, I guess it would be rude to ignore—'

'Ice cream?' she interrupted. 'But I don't have a dish.'

'Won't you catch cold?'

'Not if you warm me. Lick it off…'

'I intend to.'

From there it was a rough and tumble that saw them end up on the floor, with pizza scattered everywhere and rapidly melting ice cream coating parts of them urgently needing attention.

'It's in my hair,' Sofia laughingly complained at one point.

Swiping ice cream from his chin, he ordered, 'Stop complaining.'

'Everything's an opportunity for you,' she scolded between shrieks of hysterical pleasure.

Rolling Sofia onto her back, he loomed over her. 'Sofia Acosta, I'm asking you again, and again, and again, will you marry me?'

'Must I repeat my answer?'

'Do you want more pleasure or not?'

'Why ask when you know my answer?'

'Because last time I didn't ask, I instructed, and I'm trying to mend my ways.'

'By proposing while I'm covered in ice cream, lying naked on your kitchen table?'

'I can't think of a better time, can you?'

They stared into each other's eyes, and then Sofia's mouth began to twitch. Once she started laughing, she couldn't stop.

'I'll go down on bended knee later,' he promised.

'I'll hold you to that,' she warned as he silenced her with a kiss.

It was a long time later, after an extremely lengthy shower, that they finally made it to his bed. 'I just want you to be sure,' Sofia told him as he drew her into his arms. 'Marriage is such a huge step for you.'

'And for you, as it is for anyone,' he argued. 'I can't pretend we won't live in the spotlight, but it's up to us to make time for each other.'

'And our family,' she whispered against his mouth.

'The balancing act won't be easy,' he agreed. 'Serving our country in the full glare of publicity while maintaining a happy family life will be a challenge, but as we both thrive on challenge I don't see a problem. We'll be stronger together than we are apart.'

'You make a good case, Prince Cesar,' Sofia teased tenderly.

'I'm fighting for a woman who is worth the world to me. If you had left me, I would have regretted it for the rest of my life—and I've got too much living to do to waste time on regret.'

Sofia's eyes searched his with concern. 'A huge royal wedding with a cathedral full of people we don't even know?'

'What about that wedding on the beach you talked about?'

'You can't. You're a prince.'

'I can do anything I want to do,' he assured Sofia. 'We can have a grand ceremony in the cathedral to celebrate the birth of the first of our many children or a formal blessing in the months after our marriage. Our countrymen are romantics at heart—they're Italian,' he reminded her. 'And we won't sell them short. We'll share our lives—good and bad—so they have an insight into the human side of our royal partnership. I know my people's generosity of spirit well enough to be confident that they will applaud our decision to have a simple beachside wedding, for no other reason than it means so much to us.'

'Saying our own words in our own way, rather than repeating words written by someone who doesn't even know us,' Sofia reflected out loud. Her eyes brightened as she saw the possibility of change for the better opening out in front of them both.

'Exactly.'

'You'd do this for me?'

'I'd do anything for you,' he confirmed. 'I'm saying I love you in every way I know. I'll always respect royal traditions, but we can still do things our way, a new way, and if a wedding on the beach is what you want, a wedding on the beach is what you shall have.'

'I can't think of anything I want more than to be your wife, to stand alongside you, whatever the future brings. I love you so much,' Sofia whispered, staring up into his eyes.

The first charity polo match was brought forward. The crowd was vast. The game was fierce. Sofia and Olivia proved indispensable members of the winning team, which was naturally Team Lobos. They defeated the infamous Argentinian Team Assassin, led by past world champion Nero Caracas, by seven goals to six. Any other result would have been unacceptable, Sofia's fiercest brother Xander told Cesar without a flicker of expression on his tough, unforgiving face.

To allow the cheering fans to see many of the world's top players in action, both sides swapped different players for each chukka, so there was a huge crowd of players and their families in the cookhouse afterwards, where warm camaraderie prevailed. What had happened on the pitch stayed on the pitch, and all that mattered now were the huge sums of money raised for their favourite charities. It was the perfect time to make an announcement.

Tapping a champagne bottle, Cesar grabbed everyone's attention. As silence fell, he announced, 'Sofia and I are getting married.'

'Does Sofia know?' demanded Nero Caracas, Cesar's arch-rival and great friend, to a chorus of raucous cheers.

'She does,' Sofia shouted, coming to Cesar's side to link her arm through his. 'And you're all invited to our wedding on the beach on the beautiful island of Isla Ardente.'

Isla Ardente. Paradise on earth. That was Sofia's first impression of Cesar's private island, and it only improved in her eyes as she walked barefoot down the firm sugar-sand beach to join her life with his.

Cesar had dressed simply in a loose-fitting

white linen shirt that was striking against his tan. He had completed the ensemble with delightfully fine linen trousers in a dusky shade of taupe that would slip off as easily as he'd put them on. These things were important when you spent most of your life in tight-fitting breeches.

Sofia was wearing the wedding gown they'd chosen together. It was also flimsy and easy to remove. A dream of a dress, it was an unadorned slip of ankle-length ivory silk that moulded her body with loving attention to detail. She wore her hair down with a coronet of fresh flowers, picked that morning in the palace gardens, secured around her forehead with a floating rose-pink ribbon. Instead of a bouquet, she carried her wedding gift from Cesar. The puppy was his hound Bran's prettiest daughter. So Cesar hadn't quite kept to the rules when it came to this marriage, any more than she had.

Jess was waiting as she reached his side to take the puppy from her. Linking fingers with Sofia, Cesar brought her hand to his lips. Dipping his head, he murmured, 'I love you… How beautiful you are.' And then his lips brushed her neck, her mouth. 'I can't wait to get you alone—'

The celebrant cleared his throat abruptly, which made the unruly guests laugh, but even the minister was smiling; everyone was in the same euphoric mood.

'I do,' Sofia confirmed as the surf rustled and lapped over her naked feet.

'Time and tide wait for no man, not even a prince,' Cesar explained with a dark smile for Sofia as a groom brought up his great black stallion.

Swinging into the saddle, he lifted Sofia into his arms, and to the cheers of their guests they galloped away for some vital private time before the wedding feast began.

EPILOGUE

'WE'VE COME A long way, *piccola amata.*'

'A very long way,' Sofia agreed, smiling as she snuggled closer to Cesar. How she loved this intimacy between them. Most of all she loved the happy family they had created amidst the pomp and duty of royal life.

Currently they were staring down with the same astonished adoration they had experienced when their twins had been born three years ago. Their latest beloved newborn was a baby girl called Thea, after Sofia's mother. Thea was sister to Nico and Tino, their three-year-old sons. The boys were currently nestled on the bed alongside them, admiring the new addition to their family.

'I bought you something,' Cesar remembered, delving into the pocket of his jeans.

'Cesar, no,' Sofia protested as he brought out a night-blue velvet jewel case. She gazed lovingly at their children. 'You've given me everything I need already.'

She could never have predicted how happy they would be. The people of Ardente Sestieri celebrated their Prince's tight family unit at an annual celebration in the castle gardens each year. This year Cesar and Sofia would share the joy of a new baby with their people, and not just with a series of photographs taken by Cesar but with new portraits of the children painted by Sofia, just as soon as she was back at her easel.

The polo matches continued to raise vast sums for charity, while Sofia's retreat had developed into a worldwide charitable foundation with outreach services, and Cesar was popularly acclaimed as the most charitable and caring Prince in his country's history.

'Aren't you going to open it?' her loving husband prompted. 'The boys are waiting. We love you so much, and Nico and Tino helped me choose the gift.'

'I'll love it whatever it is,' Sofia assured them, but Tino and Nico were more interested in their baby sister curling her tiny fists around their fingers.

'Another warrior woman,' Cesar groaned.

Sofia gasped on opening the jewel box. He helped her to remove the most beautiful diamond necklace from its snug velvet nest.

She had become accustomed to wearing the priceless, heavy and opulent gems of state. Always conscious of their history, she felt humbled wearing them, but this was a different jewel, because this was a gift from Cesar's heart.

The fine gold chain held three pure blue-white diamond hearts. 'With room for more,' Cesar pointed out.

'Do you really think these three will give us the chance to add to our family?'

'You can depend on it,' he promised.

Staring into the darkly seductive eyes of a man she trusted and loved more than anything else on earth, she believed him.

* * * * *

LET'S TALK
Romance

For exclusive extracts, competitions
and special offers, find us online:

f facebook.com/millsandboon

○ @millsandboonuk

🐦 @millsandboon

Or get in touch on 0844 844 1351*

For all the latest titles coming soon,
visit millsandboon.co.uk/nextmonth

Want even more
ROMANCE?

Join our bookclub today!